Other Side of Night
Bastian & Riley

S.L. Armstrong & K. Piet

Storm Moon Press LLC
12814 University Club Drive, #102
Tampa, FL 33612

Publisher's Note

This is a work of fiction. Names, characters, places, and
incidents either are the product of the authors' imaginations
or are used fictitiously. Any resemblance to actual persons,
living or dead, events or locales is entirely coincidental.

The publisher has no control over and does not assume
responsibility for any third-party websites or their content.
The uploading and distribution of this book via the Internet
or via any other means without the permission of the
publisher is illegal and punishable by law.

Cover art by Nathie
http://www.creationwarrior.net/

ISBN-13: 978-1-937058-25-8
ISBN-10:   1-937058-25-5

Bastian

Chapter One

Bastian sat at their usual table, his eyes darting around the busy street corner. The sun had just set, and he'd made it to his standing date with Riley early. When the server asked him what he wanted, he absently ordered whatever seasonal crap the place was serving. Coffee was coffee to Bastian, especially since that damn frat party last semester, so he didn't really care what they brought. It's not like he was going to drink it anyway.

Riley came into sight across the street, and Bastian couldn't help but smile. A few months ago, Riley would have been a blur at that distance, but now he could make out every tiny detail. They'd met by chance, or so Riley thought. He'd been watching the junior since the start of the year, but when they'd bumped into each other in the quad three weeks ago, Bastian had thrown caution to the wind. He'd asked Riley out for coffee, and now they met every Thursday evening for a couple of hours before Riley had to go to work.

"Bastian," Riley said, letting the heavy book bag he carried fall to the ground with a thud. "I'm sorry if I kept you waiting."

Bastian shook his head. "I haven't been waiting long, no," he insisted. Riley smiled, and it made Bastian's heart—such as it was—skip a beat. That smile lit up the turquoise eyes that enhanced his ginger hair. Riley, Bastian thought fondly, was the quintessential redhead, and he

3

thought it was hotter than hell. "I ordered something for myself, but I didn't get you anything yet since I didn't know when you'd be coming..." God help him, was he rambling? Again?

Riley laughed and sat down. "It's all right. I like my tea really hot, so I can order when they bring yours out. How are you doing, Bastian? You don't look so pale tonight. You're feeling better?"

He loved how Riley called him Bastian. No one else had done it, but Riley had started immediately upon learning his name was Sebastian. "A little," he admitted. Yeah, he was feeling better. He'd downed a quart of pig's blood that he'd wrangled from a butcher 20 minutes away from the university. "How about you?"

"I'm all right," Riley shrugged. "Busy. Classes are hell this year, and the new schedule at Dr. Freedman's is just completely fucking with my free time."

"Night shifts can be a bitch," Bastian agreed. He'd been working them since the semester started. Luckily, he'd been able to switch around a couple classes so he could sleep in. "I'm just glad I have my studios in the late afternoon. The less sun I get, the better."

Riley ordered his tea, and then gave Bastian an odd look. "I've never met anyone with an honest-to-God sun allergy. It must make things really complicated."

"Yeah," Bastian mumbled unhappily, holding his coffee cup with both hands. Riley didn't know the half of it, and he hadn't offered up the information. It wasn't just that he had to avoid the sun; he had to be completely covered now from head to toe. It had only taken one careless morning that ended in third degree burns to teach him to cover the windows *and* every inch of skin when he went out. "It's a death sentence to the social life. People tend to stay away when you're dressed like a ninja in the middle of fucking summer."

"And that doctor friend of yours hasn't been able to help?"

Bastian shook his head. It was a simple cover story, but there was no way he was going to an actual doctor. Something was seriously wrong with him, and he knew he'd only be studied, poked and prodded, and that wasn't how he planned on spending his college career. "It's just best if I keep covered up during the day. But, hey, the sun's down and I'm not dressed from head to toe."

Riley's eyes moved over his face and upper body, an appreciative light in them. "I say it's a marked improvement," he murmured.

He had just enough blood in his system to muster up a genuine blush. He knew he was good looking. Italian genetics had gifted him with a slightly olive complexion and silky, dark hair. He'd never had any complaints until he'd had to bundle up to go to class. Compliments were a bit more difficult to come by now, but the nighttime was his sanctuary, and these meetings with Riley were a lifesaver when it came to his ego. "Thanks," he finally said, making a show out of preening his hair. He stopped when he realized just how flamboyant and ridiculous it must look. He stifled an embarrassed laugh with a large swallow of coffee.

Riley grinned at him, all boyish charm. "We really should try doing something other than meeting for tea and coffee," he said. "Maybe... a movie?"

"A movie?" Bastian couldn't believe his luck. He was a freak now, shunned by most of his old friends, but Riley was asking him out. "Like... on a date?"

"Yeah," Riley said, his pale face suffusing with color. It made that new hunger in Bastian pique with interest. "Like on a date. You. Me. A crappy, cheap movie. The dark."

Bastian laughed. "I'd love that. I haven't been on a date in a really long time."

"I haven't, either," Riley confided. He shifted, and Bastian could immediately sense his discomfort. "My ex... well, he wasn't a very nice guy, and I decided to take a break from dating."

Bastian frowned, his eyebrows knitting together. He'd known that Riley wasn't dating just from their casual conversations, but he had assumed Riley was getting a little action, maybe something without strings. Riley was hot enough for that, and it's what Bastian's M.O. had been before things got crazy. If Riley had a shitty ex, though, it probably meant he was wrong. "What happened?" he asked. "I mean, if you don't mind sharing. I don't wanna make it worse or anything but..." He let the sentence trail off and just rested his hand on Riley's in what he hoped came off as a comforting gesture.

Riley smiled, but the expression didn't make it to his eyes. Bastian much preferred the more natural, bright smile he'd been gifted with when Riley had first sat down than this new, artificial one. "Jake just wasn't a nice guy once we moved in with each other. We met in freshman year, and while he was the jealous type, I liked how much he wanted my attention."

"Jealous type?" That set off warning bells in Bastian's head.

"That's what everyone said about him." Riley set his cup aside. "I thought it was sweet. We moved in together at the start of our sophomore year. Things devolved. Jealous isn't the word I'd use to describe Jake anymore. He was *obsessive* about me. I had to tell him where I was going, who I'd be with, when I'd be back... unless he went with me, which he usually did." He sighed, eyes turning to the street. "We'd been together a few months when he hit me the first time. It went downhill from there."

Bastian swallowed thickly. "Shit."

Riley gave him a wry smile. "I moved out over the summer, just before the fall semester started. I got a new job, transferred schools, and basically uprooted my life. He wouldn't have stopped what he'd been doing."

From those words alone, and the haunted look in Riley's eyes, Bastian had a good feeling Jake hadn't just been hitting Riley. Out of respect, he didn't dig. If Riley wanted him to know, he'd tell him. "Started over?"

"I've made new friends, and I like UT better than Tennessee State," Riley said. "I have my own little apartment off campus, a job that helps with the bills, and some great professors. I think my situation was greatly improved by leaving Nashville and Jake behind."

Bastian dared to grin, wanting to lighten the mood just a little. "And you met me, the oddball of UT."

Riley laughed, shaking his head. "You may be an oddball, but you're nice and gorgeous and smart, so I can accept that you're weird."

"Good, 'cause I'd be heartbroken if you couldn't."

Silence fell between them as they sipped their drinks and watched the people passing the coffee shop. When Riley arched his neck to watch a woman with her dog at the crosswalk, murmuring that choke chains should be illegal, Bastian's gaze was drawn to the exposed flesh. He knew, just beneath a little muscle and some tissue, was a beating, pulsing artery that was full of warmth and life. It made that nagging thirst cry out, demand to be fed and sated for once, and Bastian squeezed his eyes shut.

But it was too late. He was starving. Ravenous almost. He wanted to pant, to claw at himself to stop the burning inside him. If he wasn't careful, he'd lunge right over the table, in front of dozens of witnesses, and just savage Riley, which he didn't want to do. He didn't want it, but, God help him, he did. Bastian wanted the hunger to stop, the pain to ease even for a few hours, and that dark voice in his head assured him if he'd take Riley's life...

Bastian stood up suddenly. "I have to go," he ground out, not looking at Riley. "I forgot I have to... do... something..."

"Bastian?"

Oh, Riley's voice was concerned, gentle, and Bastian wanted to look, to explain, but he just shook his head. "I'll call you tomorrow night? We can decide what movie and day and all that shit, okay? I just *really* have to go. Now."

He could see Riley nodding in his peripheral vision. "All right, Bastian. Call my cell. I'm working tomorrow night."

Bastian nodded, the movement jerky and painful. "Tomorrow night. Your cell. I'll call around eight." He didn't even say goodbye. He didn't even let himself register the disappointed 'goodbye' Riley threw in his direction. Bastian simply took off across the street. He wanted as much space between Riley and him as he could get. He needed to breathe. He needed to get his head on straight. Had the pig's blood just not been enough? It had been a whole damn quart!

"Fuck," he hissed under his breath. He headed toward campus and his lonely dorm room. If the need didn't ease soon, he'd stop off at the grocery store. Maybe they'd have something... like a six-pack of people.

He laughed, and the desperate edge to it drew stares from the men and women he passed, but he didn't care. He felt insane; they might as well think he was, too. Bastian's mind turned again and again to Riley's throat and what coursed just under the skin. He stopped for a moment and took several deep breaths. When he opened his eyes, he looked around. He needed to find someplace where he could get his fix.

Fix. He sounded like an addict, but this wasn't an addiction. He couldn't kick the need for blood any more than a normal person could kick the need for water. It was a dry scrape through his veins, a twisting in his gut. His tongue was thick and dry in his mouth. Every person he passed tugged at his fraying control. Bastian was dangerous. He knew that in a sudden, frightening revelation. It was just like the first night, that first and only kill. If he didn't do something now, someone was going to get hurt.

There was a Fresh Market on Kingston Pike. That wasn't too far from where he was now. Bastian ducked his head and took off down the street at a jog. It wouldn't take him too long, and there was no denying the truth. If he'd been that tempted to rip Riley's throat out—someone he wanted to date and know and, hell, maybe even fuck—then the hunger was out of control. One quart of pig's blood a week wasn't cutting it anymore.

He often wondered if human blood would satisfy him longer, but the thought of giving in to that urge turned his stomach. He shook his head as an image of Riley rose up in his mind. No, not Riley. Not anyone. Never again.

Chapter Two

Bastian kicked the door of his mini-fridge closed and wiped his mouth with the back of his hand. He'd started drinking extra blood and even carried around a couple energy shot bottles of it when he'd go out for his classes or job. Those dangerous urges had become a little less severe for it, but it was still disturbing to greet the day with a mug of blood instead of coffee.

He ran a hand through his wet hair before crossing to the mirror and sink next to the door of the bathroom adjoining his room with his suite-mates'. The shower was tiny, but at least the water wasn't exactly on his dime. He was spending more time in his showers than he could ever remember enjoying in the past. It wasn't so much that he felt dirty or sweaty, especially now that autumn was setting in, but he just couldn't get enough of the heat.

He snorted to himself, glancing over his reflection. Bundle up to go outside and feel like he's being roasted like a baked potato wrapped in foil, or dress normal and feel like the only way he'd warm up was a scalding hot bath. It was a strange back and forth that he forced himself to laugh at. If he couldn't laugh at himself, he'd probably go batshit insane.

After combing his hair back from his face, he grabbed his toothbrush and loaded it with toothpaste. Time to get the taste and smell of blood out of his mouth. He had that movie date with Riley, and even if he didn't expect to score, he didn't want to taste like some dead animal if they kissed. That would be worse than garlic breath and smelly dog rolled into one. Riley probably got enough of pet smells in his vet classes; he definitely didn't need that from Bastian on a date.

Wetting the brush, he set to scrubbing his teeth. They'd felt funny over the last week, even kind of loose, but he was an adult. He'd lost all his baby teeth years ago, and he'd even had his wisdom teeth yanked before he hit college. There was no reason for him to have unstable teeth. He ate well and hadn't taken any blows to the face.

He frowned as he moved his brush over the teeth again, experimentally putting more pressure on them in an up-down motion. They moved again and he felt his pulse pick up. A little more pressure and – *crack*.

Bastian's eyes widened, and he pulled his brush out, his lips puckered to keep all the suds of the toothpaste in his mouth. He cautiously ran his tongue up near the gum surrounding the tooth and the sickening crackle repeated, sending a tremor of panic down his spine. He swiped his tongue over to the opposite side, where he'd noticed another wobbling tooth, and not only did another crack ring in his ears, but a shooting pain stabbed at his upper jaw. The unmistakable flavor of blood streaked over his tongue, and he whimpered as panic raced through him.

He clenched his toothbrush in a vice-like grip and sucked just a little to gather the spit and minty suds. Leaning over the sink, he spat, and felt his heart stop dead in his chest. The tiny clatter against the sink was terrifyingly delicate. Amid the blood-tinged toothpaste were two of his teeth.

In that instant, the world went from standing utterly still to spinning at breakneck speeds. Bastian couldn't tear his eyes away from the long, bloody lengths of his teeth in the sink, even as he dropped his toothbrush and began panting wildly. He managed to bring his shaking hands up to his mouth and, pulling back his lips, he followed his gums from his two front teeth outward.

Both fingers found the voids in his mouth at the same moment, and he let out a panicked yelp. It wasn't just his imagination. His teeth were gone. His teeth had fucking fallen out! His heart pounded in his chest, and his fingertips pressed into the holes, but instead of finding them empty, they encountered needle-like points in the gums. His hands jerked out of his mouth, and he hissed as pain shot up from the sensitive pads of his index fingers.

Bastian's eyes darted to the pricked tips of his fingers. They then flashed to the mirror. He stepped close, pulled his lip back again, and tilted his head. He could make out two sharp points, gleaming white in the spaces where his canines had been.

Pressure built in his chest as he stared and panted, and it erupted from him a few seconds later in a harsh shout. Once the first sound was out of him, it was like he couldn't stay silent. He screamed at his reflection, but he couldn't keep looking at himself. His eyes looked everywhere at once, filling his head with visions of blood, lost teeth, and the new buds that were taking their place.

Fangs. Fucking hell, he was growing *fangs*!

"Fuck!" he cried, gripping the countertop as he slowly sank to the floor. He released his hold an instant later, though, and gave up on trying to stay upright in favor of hugging his knees to his chest. Whimpering, he tried not to think about what was happening to him, but even when he tried to hide his face against his knees, the sight of those teeth was burned into the backs of his eyes.

What the fuck was happening? First the blood and dangerous thoughts, and then the sunlight bullshit, and now *this*? He'd been able to tell himself he'd just gotten some fucked up STD from that one night stand a few months back. He'd told himself that over and over until he started to believe it and move on, dealing with whatever he had, but now his body was changing, too.

He couldn't lie to himself now. He wanted to—God, how he wanted to—but whether he liked it or not, he had a damned good word for what was going on. His eyes teared up, and he sobbed into his knees, willing away all the things that had gone wrong the last three months. Bastian didn't want this, didn't need shit like this on top of everything else in his life.

The ring from his cell phone was harsh to his ears and made his head jerk up in fear. His eyes darted to the nightstand next to his bed, and panic washed through him once more when he recognized the tune and picture flashing on the screen.

His boss. Damn it!

He was on his feet in an instant, and even when he had the phone in his hand, he paced. He couldn't answer like this. His nose was stuffed up, his teeth missing, and he just knew there would be that edge of panic to his voice. Forcing himself to stand still, he concentrated solely on his breathing for a few seconds. Deep breath in, slow exhale. In and out.

The phone beeped. He'd missed the call. It was just as well. The one he needed to call right now wasn't his boss but Riley. He could just call in sick to work, no big deal, but Riley...

Bastian felt his throat clench and his heart sink. His first date in ages and now this had to happen.

He tried to think of something good to say, maybe a lie that would lighten the blow, but his mind went blank. It was no use trying to rehearse. He brought the phone to his ear without opening his eyes and pressed the speed-dial button for Riley's cell phone.

The country song Riley had instead of the ringing tones usually made him smile when he would call, but now it was like some sort of sick dirge, mocking his grief with its upbeat lyrics. It cut off suddenly to Riley's voice telling him to leave a message. He wasn't sure if he was relieved or not.

"Hi, Riley," he managed to choke out after the beep, his voice uneven, but not nearly as watery or panicked as he'd feared. It was, though, just as awkward as he'd thought to speak without his teeth in place. Bastian knew he wouldn't be able to completely fool Riley, so full-on lying was out of the question. He clenched his jaw for a moment in the effort not to cry anymore, but it made the ache of his gums more pronounced, and he stifled a whimper.

"I can't make it tonight," he blurted out, speaking quickly, as if that would make things better. "I can't make it out for a while. I'm really sorry, but something's just..." His voice faded as he stumbled over his words, unable to just tell Riley what was happening. "I can't go out right now. I'll call you when I get some free time again and I'm feeling up for it, promise."

It didn't feel right to say goodbye over the phone, so he just hung up. A sudden surge of anger made him want to throw his phone against the far wall and see it smashed to pieces. As soon as the anger subsided, the grief settled into his bones. He wasn't like Riley anymore. He wanted to be, wanted to just smile and laugh and be happy, but that asshole at the frat party had changed everything.

That asshole had changed *him*.

He tossed the phone to his bed and went back to his small sink and mirror. The bubbles had faded in the sink, leaving behind a pinkish residue and his two teeth. The fear was still there, making his heart pound, but the pit in his stomach was a knot of loss.

He looked up at his reflection, at the blood and toothpaste caked at the sides of his mouth, and grimaced. His sinuses stung again with oncoming tears, and he ducked his head to rinse his mouth.

What the hell was he going to do now?

It took Bastian three weeks before he could muster up the courage to call Riley. Three agonizing weeks where he watched his teeth slowly grow in. They weren't really noticeable, but *he* knew they were there. Sharp and cumbersome and inhuman. It was the inhuman part that continued to sit uneasily with him even as he made his way to the coffee shop to meet Riley.

He'd done some serious groveling. Riley had been pissed. Bastian couldn't blame him. He'd canceled their date, and then dropped off the face of the planet. Riley had called him six times before giving up, and Bastian had listened to his voice mail over and over, listening to the concern, the confusion. In the final message, he'd heard resignation and a hint of resentment, even though Riley had wished him well. It had been the note of hurt, genuine hurt, he'd heard in those last words that had spurred him into action. If he didn't act now, he'd lose any chance he might have had with Riley.

And, damn, he wanted Riley. He wanted him badly. Sex was on his mind frequently, but so was blood. Bastian's fantasies had grown disturbing over the passing weeks. The scenes his mind painted were hot, Riley on his knees in front of him or bent over the nearest surface, but just as he was about to come, the scenes always took a bloody turn. He'd come with the violent image of pounding in and out of Riley's body while his new fangs sank into Riley's throat, blood splashing over his tongue.

Bastian paused at the light and waited for the crosswalk light to change. He closed his eyes and took a deep breath of the cold, late fall air, trying to clear his mind of those erotic, deadly fantasies.

Yeah, he'd groveled.

"Hey, Riley."

Silence on the other end of the phone line, and then, "Sebastian."

Bastian cringed. Riley had only called him Sebastian once, right after they'd met, and then decided 'Bastian' suited him better. The distance that one word put between them hurt, and that hurt shocked Bastian. They'd been out for a handful of casual meetings at a coffee house, and he was already thoroughly infatuated with the man. "I... uh... meant to call before now, but I've been... under the weather."

"So under the weather you couldn't return a single phone call?" Riley's voice was annoyed, and Bastian clung to that annoyance. Annoyance meant he still mattered.

"I fucked up. I canceled last minute with a pretty lame excuse, but, honest, Riley, I've had a shitty month, and

you got the raw end of that. I'm sorry. Let me make it up to you?" Silence again, and Bastian rubbed the bridge of his nose. "Please?"

There was yet more silence before Riley finally relented. "How about we meet at the coffee shop Wednesday night? I have to work tomorrow, Thursday, and Friday."

Bastian grinned. "Wednesday night is perfect."

"If you stand me up again, there won't be another chance, Bastian."

He closed his eyes. There was the undercurrent of anger and hurt still in Riley's words, but he'd called him Bastian. "I won't. Eight good?"

"Eight's perfect."

It was seven-thirty, but Bastian had figured it was better to be early than late. He didn't want Riley to think— even for a moment—that he'd stood him up. This was his one and only chance to make things right, and Bastian wasn't about to fuck it up, too.

The light changed and Bastian crossed over to the coffee shop. He grabbed their usual table, ordered his usual coffee, and waited. Bastian wasn't typically an impatient sort of guy, but tonight, he couldn't sit still. His eyes darted left and right, watching the street, waiting for any sign of fiery red hair. Bastian waited until quarter after eight before he began to worry.

Maybe Riley was paying him back? He deserved it. He had been offered a golden opportunity. Riley had been that single chance to shed the promiscuity that had led him to this new state of being. A lover, steady and understanding, sexy as hell, brilliant, and absolutely amazing, had slipped through his fingers because he was an utter asshole. Bastian shoved his hands into his hair and leaned forward, bracing his elbows on his thighs. Christ, what had he done? What had he lost before even getting to appreciate it?

"You look like a man in need of a serious vacation."

Bastian looked up, his heart beating quickly as he took in the sight of Riley. Riley, tall and beautiful and there. Late, but there, a rueful smile curving his luscious mouth. "Like I said, it's been a long month," he choked out.

"Has it?" Riley sat down, tucking his book bag under his chair. "I wouldn't know. You didn't call."

"I'm sorry." Bastian had drunk a good amount of the cow's blood from his fridge before heading out, and he was only sort of surprised to feel his cheeks heat slightly with a flush. It had been too long since he'd last felt himself blush. "I really am. I wanted to call, but shit came up and I... didn't know how to explain the changes in my life to you."

"Changes? Did you knock a girl up? Decide you weren't gay? Get married?" Riley ordered his tea latte, and then turned sharp, bright eyes on him. "Come on, Bastian, what was it? Food poisoning? Cut off a finger? Lose your scholarship?"

Bastian shook his head. "Okay, maybe not as dire as anything like that, but..."

"But *what*?"

How was he supposed to explain this? *Should* he explain it? They hadn't even gone out on their first date! Before he announced he was pretty sure he was a vampire, they should have at least managed three dates, right? Bastian sighed. "I just got really hung up on some of my classes while coming down with something. If I wasn't studying, I was in bed. I'm sorry I canceled last minute on you. Do you think we could try again?"

Riley eyed him, sipping his tea. "You going to be sick Sunday night?"

Bastian felt a hesitant smile tug at the corners of his lips. "No."

"You want to try that dinner and a movie thing again?"

"Yes." Bastian tried to be cool about, not seem too eager, but Riley's soft laugh told him he'd failed. "Yes, I want to try it again. I really, *really* want to."

Riley smiled, that bright and beautiful expression that lit up his face. "Good, 'cause I want to, too." The smile faded a little. "Don't do that again. Call me back. I was worried as hell."

Bastian shifted his chair over and laced his fingers with Riley's. It was natural, easy and comfortable. His smile was more reserved, hiding his new teeth as much as he could. "I can't say it enough. I'm sorry. It was thoughtless–"

"Yes."

"And rude–"

"Yes."

"And–"

Riley pressed a finger to Bastian's lips. "Yes." He leaned in, his eyes darting to Bastian's lips for a moment before his finger slid away, over his chin and down his throat. "As much as I'd like hear you beg for forgiveness the rest of the evening, I think you've done enough. You screwed up. Don't do it again, 'kay?"

Bastian nodded, and he knew what they were going to do. He knew he shouldn't, he knew he should wait, but Riley was there, so close, and he smelled so damn good. Bastian leaned a little closer and murmured, "I want to kiss you."

"You *want* to?" Riley's eyes sparkled. "Wanting is such an unpleasant state to be in."

Bastian couldn't help the laugh that filled his throat. "It is. I think it's time to remedy it."

The kiss was simple, but Bastian knew he'd remember it for the rest of his life. Riley's lips were soft, pliant, and Bastian could smell the lingering soap on his skin from a shower he'd taken that day. It was fresh, something citrusy. There was also the scent of books and ink and cat. He slid his hand into Riley's hair and it was just as soft and thick as he'd imagined it to be. Bastian pressed lingering kisses to Riley's lips, their lips only slightly parted, and his cock hardened when Riley uttered that first melodic moan. He brushed his lips over Riley's a final time, and then hovered there, his breath mingling with Riley's as he tried to sort out which was up and which was down after such a spectacular, almost-chaste kiss.

Riley's eyes opened slowly, and Bastian just stared into them. It wasn't an awkward silence. It wasn't uncomfortable. In those blue-green eyes, Bastian saw his own arousal reflected. The kiss had done as much for Riley as it had for him, and that gave him the confidence he needed. He smiled his careful smile. "Do you have anywhere you have to be right now?"

"No," Riley breathed. "I'm yours until the shop closes. I have a late class tomorrow."

Bastian wanted to grin. He wanted to show his teeth in a pleased, satisfied smile. Instead, he combed his fingers through Riley's hair. "I'm glad, because I want to know everything I can about you."

"That's a tall order."

Bastian kissed Riley again, brief and sweet. "We have time."

Riley relaxed in his chair, holding his cup in his hands. "Where should I start?"

Bastian got comfortable in his own chair and ordered another coffee. "At the beginning," he said simply.

Chapter Three

"I'm telling you," Riley said as they exited the theater, "Brad Pitt can out-charm Channing Tatum any day."

Bastian laughed. "Maybe for now, but Pitt's got some years on Tatum. I think he'd better watch his back."

Riley shook his head. "No contest. Brad can act well. Channing? He's a flavor-of-the-month actor. Hollywood will get tired of him before he ever has a chance of deepening his mediocre acting skills."

"You think so?" Bastian wrapped his arm comfortably around Riley's waist. He'd lost count of how many dates they'd been on, but the Sunday evening dinner-and-a-movie routine had quickly replaced the casual-coffee-shop-meet-up. Bastian really looked forward to these moments that were all about *them* and little else. On these dates, Bastian felt almost human again. And, to his enjoyment, each date ended with a series of those sweet, semi-chaste kisses he'd come to crave from Riley. "I think you're underestimating his appeal."

Riley paused on the dark street to smile down at him. "Am I underestimating your appeal?"

Bastian smirked. "No, you're underestimating *yours*. The asshole in the front row only had eyes for you, which was why he was being obnoxious."

"No, he wasn't." Riley tugged him along. "He was just being a jerk."

"Uh-huh." Riley's modesty really turned Bastian on, made him think highly of the redhead. "How's Cameron?"

Riley's eldest sister was pregnant with twins, and she was having some trouble with her blood pressure. Bastian had learned everything he could about Riley's family in the first two weeks they'd been dating. He longed for that sort of large family that was almost picturesque.

"She's all right. On bed rest until the C-section." Riley's arm slipped around him as they walked down the sidewalk. "The twins aren't in any distress yet, but they think she'll need to deliver at least eight weeks early. Her blood pressure just won't stabilize."

"That isn't good," Bastian murmured.

"No, but I try not to think about it too much."

Bastian frowned as he looked at Riley. "How can you not think about it?"

Riley looked up at the dark sky. "It's just something I do. It's... it's like I put it into a little box and stick it on a shelf in my mind. I can't really help Cameron, and worrying about it endlessly would make it impossible for me to concentrate on school and work. So, I put it aside, and when I have the time and emotional fortitude, I pull out the box and deal with it." He looked back at Riley with a smile. "It's usually then that I do my little freak outs, but I need to have the time and energy."

"So, you compartmentalize everything?" What an odd way of handling life, but Bastian had to admit that it would have made things infinitely easier for him if he'd been able to do the same thing. "Have you done it your whole life?"

They began to walk again, and Riley nodded. "Yep. Cameron and Henry don't, but Mom does, and I guess I learned it from her."

Bastian shook his head, tightening his arm around Riley. "Well, I'm sure Cameron's strong enough for all three of them." He took a deep breath and let it out slowly. "On my aunt's farm, I know that the early births were some of the hardest. A lot of the calves didn't make it."

Riley tilted his head. "You lived on a farm?"

"For nearly a decade," Bastian chuckled. "It was all right, I guess, but I never really felt at home with my aunt, uncle, and cousins. I was almost completely useless when it came to helping out around the place, so I always got the shitty chores. I started up with carpentry there, though, and that's how I got into sculpting. They never really understood the whole art thing and hated that I'd skip my chores to do it, so I always felt kind of isolated."

Riley bit his lip. "What happened to your parents?"

Bastian stiffened under Riley's arm. They hadn't really talked about his folks, and he'd been okay with that. He let out a long, slow breath. "Mom and Dad worked in the same building." He wet his lips as they turned down the street that would lead them to Riley's apartment. "We lived in a pretty rough area of New York. During the day, my Grandpa would watch me after school. Dad would pick me up and walk me home in the evening while Mom made dinner."

God, it was so long ago, but he could still hear his father's voice, smell his mother's perfume. His heart ached with the memory of being happy even with only the barest of things. The essentials, his father had told him, were all a family needed: a home, food, and each other. He'd never forgotten that. He never would.

"There was a fire. I didn't know much about it until I was sixteen, and even then I had to look it up. Someone had been smoking in the lower level of the building. A fire caught, and the building hadn't been up to code. Not much in that neighborhood was." Bastian clenched his jaw for a moment, and Riley stopped them on the stoop of the converted colonial that housed four apartments.

Riley's face was so serious. "How old were you?"

"Six." Bastian brushed his fingers over Riley's cheek. "My birthday had been two weeks before they died. They had sprung for a bakery cake in the shape of a turtle and bought my favorite ice cream."

"Oh, Bastian," Riley whispered.

Bastian tried to smile, but he knew it wouldn't reach his eyes. "I don't really talk about them often. It's not something most people want to hear, y'know?"

Riley tilted his head, rubbing his cheek against Bastian's palm. "I want to hear it. It's a part of you. I know way too little while you know just about everything about me."

It was so tender and genuine. Bastian had never been around someone who honestly cared like Riley did. It made a part of him deep inside feel warm and safe, two things he hadn't felt much in the last few months. "Are you planning on a full investigation inside, or...?" His voice faded as he glanced from Riley to the door and back with a more heartfelt smile. Maybe it was cocky to think he'd be invited in, but he could hope, right?

"You've been such a gentleman," Riley teased. Bastian was grateful that the topic of his parents had been dropped for the moment. "Maybe I should invite you in for a night cap, hmm?"

Bastian chuckled, the tension in his shoulders easing. "I wouldn't insult you by saying no."

Riley led him through the door and into the interior hallway. How many Sundays had he stood here, kissed Riley goodnight, and been sent away? But tonight... Tonight, he was being invited in. He'd had a large glass of blood before the date, and he had even nuzzled Riley's throat in the theater with no urge to bite, so Bastian was marking this as a safe, exciting moment. It was a step forward with Riley, who was still so gun-shy after the ex.

The door opened and Riley beckoned him in. The living room was small, tidy, and on the couch was a fluffy white cat. That was where the constant scent of cat came from. The cat rose, stretched, and eagerly jumped down to pad over to Riley, winding around his feet. Riley picked the cat and smiled at Bastian.

"This is Zoe. Zoe, this is Bastian," he said, scritching under Zoe's chin.

Bastian joined in by rubbing Zoe's forehead and scratching behind her ears. "Hey, Zoe," he greeted with a smile before holding his arms open. "Can I hold her?"

Riley flashed him a wary look but handed Zoe over carefully. Bastian supported her hind paws and leaned her against his chest, freeing up his other hand for a few introductory pets and a very thorough scritch. Zoe struggled a little at first, but his touch won her over, and she nuzzled his coat. He'd have white fur all over him after this, but as Zoe's purr rumbled up at him, he knew he couldn't care less.

Riley grinned then. "She likes you."

Bastian wanted to return the grin, but settled instead on smirking. "Does she like everyone you bring home?"

"Not everyone." Riley chuckled. "And definitely not when they pick her up."

Bastian hummed happily, enjoying the warmth of Zoe against his hands. He glanced between cat and owner as Riley took off his coat. "Did Zoe like Jake at all?" he asked cautiously.

Riley paused, coat halfway to the hook by his door, and then murmured, "No. She hid from the time he would come home to the time he left the apartment again. She hid for about a month after I moved, but I think she's finally realized Jake isn't coming here. Ever."

Bastian hugged Zoe a little tighter, but he eased off when she meowed a protest up at him. "Sorry," he murmured, both to Zoe and Riley. "I guess her liking me bodes well, then." It was also a little reassuring. Jake had been a real asshole, and Zoe had picked up on that with that special sense animals sometimes had. He was growing fangs and drinking blood, but Zoe trusted him.

Zoe hopped down and prissily stalked into the kitchen. Riley laughed softly. "You are no match for her food dish."

"Well, we did meet up right after your classes, so she's gone hungry all day. Such a bad owner," Bastian tsked.

Riley rolled his eyes. "Did you not see the size of her? She is hardly starving."

Still, Riley disappeared into the kitchen, and Bastian took a moment to shed his coat and look around.

It was a simple living space. A couch. A dented coffee table that had seen better days. The quilt thrown over the back of the couch was definitely homemade, and Bastian could just imagine Riley's mom sending him off to school with it. There was a small television stand with a modest television perched atop it. What dominated the room were the half-dozen tall bookcases, all packed with books.

Bastian stepped closer to the nearest shelf. It was full of textbooks. Veterinarian texts, books about various animals, biology, sociology, human studies, and two chemistry books. For a moment, embarrassment rolled through him. Compared to how well-read Riley was, he truly was some dumb hick off a lonely dairy farm.

Riley poked his head around the kitchen door frame. "What would you like to drink? I have red wine, which could actually be red wine vinegar by now, or beer."

"Lets give the wine a go. I haven't had wine in a long time. Beer's fine if that doesn't work." He had sort of avoided it after he'd left the whole frat party scene, but had the feeling sharing one with Riley wouldn't quite end like it had for him last time. It wasn't like someone was going to jump him here. A smile slowly curved his lips. The one who could jump him here would be Riley, and he wouldn't mind that one bit.

Riley gave him a peculiar look, and the slipped back into the dimness of the kitchen. "Wine it is!"

Bastian drew a finger down a book about horses. "You read a lot?"

"No," Riley called out. "I just collect books."

"Ha-ha," Bastian said. He smiled to himself. "I can't believe you've read all these."

Riley reappeared with two glasses of deep red wine. "There are also full bookcases in my bedroom and the guest room."

"Damn," Bastian muttered, awed by the sheer amount of books. He took his glass of wine before sitting down on the couch, making sure there was plenty of space for Riley to sit beside him without feeling crowded. He didn't want to fuck things up by coming on too strong, and he was seriously hoping to share more than just a simple goodnight kiss with Riley tonight. He sipped his wine, and the flavor unfolded pleasantly on his tongue. "Not bad."

"It's an inexpensive bottle," Riley confided, taking a sip of his wine as well. "I blow most of my budget on books. I love to read. I love to learn. I'm jealous you grew up on a farm, even if it seems like you weren't happy there."

"I wasn't *un*happy, but it wasn't ever home." Bastian stared into his glass, running his tongue lightly over his new fangs. Had he ever found home? He could only vaguely remember that warm, safe feeling with his mother and father, but even that was suspect. It could simply be the romanticized memories of a child longing for his parents. "I wasn't useful on the farm until I took up woodworking in high school. You saw how I handled Zoe? That's about my expertise with animals."

Riley laughed, patting Bastian's thigh. The heat of Riley's hand excited Bastian, drew attention to how alive Riley was. "We all have our specialties, what we were supposed to do in life. Mine was helping animals. Yours was art. One isn't greater than the other. I haven't an artistic bone in my body."

"Oh, come on. That isn't true," Bastian protested halfheartedly. His attention was easily drawn to Riley's wrist, and then up to his neck, where he could see the skin pulsing. He could almost hear the rush of blood, and even though that strange thirst didn't flare to life, he still caught his mouth watering. He forced himself to look away and took a large gulp of his wine.

Riley seemed, thankfully, oblivious. "Yes, it is. I can't even *pick* art, that's how bad I am artistically."

"Next time you want to buy a piece or something, you can take me along," Bastian suggested. It would be a break from their schedule of movie dates, but it would be familiar territory for him. "We'd be able to figure out your tastes and maybe find the right piece for you. And if nothing's just right, I might be able to make something for you myself, work it into my school projects and–" He cut himself off and rested his forehead in his palm.

"What?" Riley frowned. "Why did you stop?"

Bastian chuckled. "'Cause I'm rambling and making myself look stupid."

Riley smiled and set his wine glass aside. "What makes you think that?"

"I'm sitting here surrounded by hundreds of books you've read, and all I know is art. I haven't had a relationship in a really long time, so I keep getting nervous, which makes me ramble and take myself too seriously because I'm trying to impress you and..." His voice trailed off so he could take a breath, but instead of starting up again, he just gestured with his wine glass. "See?"

Riley took Bastian's glass from him and set it on the coffee table. Within a blink of an eye, his lap was suddenly full of Riley. He looked up into Riley face, flushed from the wine, and that hunger of his threatened to wake. He focused instead on Riley's lips, which were now moving.

"You don't need to impress me, Bastian," Riley whispered, wrapping his arms around Bastian's neck. "You impressed me when you begged to make things right between us, and then kept your word."

The slightest hint of heat pooled at his own cheeks, and he licked his lips unconsciously. "You invited me inside," he breathed, his arms hesitantly wrapping around Riley's waist. "Are you inviting me to stay?"

"Stay for the night, you mean?"

Bastian nodded. "How far are we about to go?" Because even deeper kissing was something they hadn't done, much less what he guessed Riley was offering. He had to be sure, and even then, it meant things were getting serious.

Riley licked his lips, uncertainty darkening his eyes. "I don't just fuck around. Sex is important to me. I know we have different opinions on that, but... for now, how do you feel about making out? Touching over our clothes?"

Bastian couldn't help but moan softly at the prospect. "Oh, I feel good about that. I feel *damn* good about that. I don't want to just fuck around either." He'd stopped fucking around once he'd been forced to face and live with one huge consequence of it. The thought sobered him, and he looked up into Riley's eyes as he cupped a freckled cheek with his hand. "I like the direction we're going, and trust me, I really want to make out with you." He shifted a little in his seat. "I just... There's something you need to know first."

"What?" Riley asked as he dipped his head down and nuzzled at Bastian's throat.

Bastian gasped, and his pulse jumped in his throat. God, when had it become so sensitive? For a few seconds, he completely forgot what he was about to say and just held Riley closer, eager for another brush of those lips. His mouth was dry, and as he licked his lips, he was reminded of his fangs. He couldn't tell Riley the truth, not all of it. Not while Riley was so close and relaxed. If he ruined this moment, he'd never forgive himself.

Swallowing thickly, he nudged Riley's face up. "I have sharp teeth," he blurted out, his voice a little breathy.

Riley smiled, rocking against Bastian a little, and goddamn, it was wonderful. That smile, the movement against him, it made Bastian's head spin. All he really wanted to do was kiss the man, grope him, feel him, drink him down—no, that path led to nothing but bloody fantasies, and he wasn't about to do that here and now.

"Sharp teeth?" Riley brought his face closer to Bastian's. "Like a big, bad wolf?"

It didn't matter how cheesy that line was. Riley delivered it just as their lips brushed together, and Bastian groaned. "Yeah, like a big, bad wolf," he whispered.

Riley drew the tip of his tongue along Bastian's lower lip. "I can handle that."

The slick tease of Riley's tongue sent a shiver down Bastian's spine. His heart raced as his hand moved from Riley's hip to cup the back of his head. When their tongues met, all thoughts of worry fled his mind. The winey, sweet taste of Riley filled his senses. Bastian groaned, pulling Riley closer, and he all but devoured Riley's mouth. He didn't care about his teeth. He didn't care about the blood waiting at home in his fridge. What he cared about, what he wanted, was right here in his lap.

Riley rubbed against him, and Bastian's attention was drawn to how hard Riley was against him. Riley would be hot and hard in his hand, he just knew it. He wanted to confirm it. Bastian wanted to stroke Riley, send him screaming as he came over his fist. Bastian's tongue sank deeper into Riley's mouth, wet and eager, their bodies moving to a rhythm neither thought about. He let go of Riley's head and took hold of his ass, squeezing the shifting muscles. Riley pulled back to moan and duck his head, and those damp lips latched onto his throat. Bastian bucked, a choked cry rasping through his throat, and he was actually afraid he'd cream his jeans.

Riley hummed against Bastian's neck. Then, he started sucking, and fuck if Bastian didn't lose his mind. He dug his nails into Riley's jeans, his body tense. Every nip and suckle to his throat wore down his sense of restraint. Riley lifted his head for a few seconds, and Bastian let loose a groan of relief. There was no way he was going to come yet. Coming meant the fun was over, and he couldn't let that happen. Not when they were just getting started.

The tingle that had started at the base of his spine receded after a few seconds. By the time Riley raked his teeth over his pulse and nudged his chin, resistance was the furthest thing from his mind. Bastian arched his neck, a thrill running through him as Riley's lips traced the lines of his throat. Any other sensation faded when Riley sucked hard over his pounding pulse. He couldn't even hear his own cry. He barely felt the rasp of their jeans as he squirmed. Riley's lips were the only thing Bastian was aware of. Those lips, that aching pressure, and the way his pulse throbbed closer and closer to the surface. The blood was a caged force trying to break free, so close to escaping his skin...

The sudden loss of Riley's mouth pulled a desperate cry from him. The room swayed in his vision. Riley was breathing just as hard and fast as he was. Riley's pulse raged beneath flushed skin. Bastian wasn't even sure how he knew it, but instinct told him it was good. It was right. He gripped Riley's hips and bucked as he twisted their bodies. In moments, Bastian pressed Riley into the worn cushions of the sofa and settled between his legs. Denim protected them, was a rough reminder that he could taste, but not have. The sight of Riley's swollen lips and flushed face made him grin. He didn't give a shit if Riley saw his teeth now. He rocked his hips forward, ground their groins together. His moan twined with Riley's, the tease and promise that motion offered them both mind-blowing.

"God, you feel so good," Riley panted.

Bastian nosed Riley's chin upward, his lips brushing along Riley's throat for the first time. Riley sighed, a fluttering, beautiful sound, and the feel of Riley's arms around his neck, pulling him closer, was Heaven. "So do you," he muttered. He bit gently at the delicate, pale skin. Careful, he was so careful now, even as he burned inside. Bastian rocked against Riley, their lips meeting again in kiss after kiss, wet and hungry. It would be enough, even if it left them aching in the end.

Chapter Four

It had been a compromise, and one Bastian had been a little uncomfortable with. Riley's friends had wanted to meet him. After six months, Bastian couldn't blame them, and he couldn't think of any more excuses to offer Riley to put them off. If he did, it was going to be lame, and Riley would give him that look.

He hated that look.

It said, 'Are you ashamed to be with me?' even as Riley smiled and let the topic pass. Last week, though, Riley had slid into his lap after a late-night movie. They'd kissed. Just as he'd managed to slide Riley's shirt off—which was as far as Riley would go, and Bastian didn't push—Riley had sprung the trap.

A lick up his throat, a whispered request, and Bastian had stood no chance. He'd worked for his pleasure that night, which left him chafed the next day, and had agreed to a game night. Bastian sat on the couch as he watched Riley rush about, setting up, putting a leaf in his table, putting out food, and grabbing the Munchkin box.

"Munchkin?" Bastian stood up. "What the hell is Munchkin?"

Riley smiled brightly. "It's a card game... sort of. We'll explain it to you."

Bastian opened up the box and picked up one of the decks. "These aren't playing cards."

"Nope." Riley plucked the deck out of his hand and put it back in the box. "Can you feed Zoe while I grab the drinks? Stephen, Matt, and Cheryl will be here any minute."

"If you promise to make mine a double shot of vodka," Bastian tried.

"No," Riley said, throwing a halfhearted glare his way. It was no use, though. Riley was on cloud nine and annoyance was impossible to affect. "You'll be fine. Now," he grabbed a tin of cat food and tossed it to Bastian, "feed Zoe."

Bastian caught the tin and tapped his fingers against the metal as he crossed to the corner cabinet. He snatched up the glazed food dish he had spun in his pottery class for Zoe. It had been a fun little surprise for Riley. No special occasion, just a little gift to show he cared. He'd been doing that a lot over the last few months. It was a lot different from his previous relationships. Which, if he were honest, hadn't really been relationships, just long bouts of fucking.

"Zoe!" He pulled the top off the cat food with a scrape. A distant thud and Zoe darted into the kitchen, her collar jingling cheerfully as she meowed up at him. He hummed happily at the silky feel of her as she curled around his legs. He crouched but held the bowl with her food just out of reach. "Remember our deal," he murmured to the cat. "If I give you the signal, you go into the bedroom and yowl so I can make an escape to check on you. Got it?" Zoe licked her chops and climbed up his knee, trying to get to the food. "So much for having an ally in you." He chuckled and set the bowl down. He gave her a quick scratch, and then stood to watch Riley again.

Riley wrapped his arms around Bastian's waist and bent his head to brush his lips against Bastian's. "Is it so bad to spend some time with my friends?"

"No," Bastian said. He slid his hands up Riley's chest. "But you know I don't do much social stuff. Not since freshman year."

"I know, which is why you need to ease back in." Riley kissed him softly, briefly. "My friends won't bite."

Bastian snorted. "Yeah, but I might."

Riley nipped his lower lip just as the doorbell rang. "Relax. Everything will be fine." He kissed Bastian once more, and then practically bounced to the door. He threw it open, laughing as his friends piled in, all four of them talking excitedly at each other.

Bastian shifted on his feet. He was out of place. They were all old friends, and they were comfortable in Riley's space. It had taken him two months before he'd felt he had the right explore Riley's apartment. Cheryl turned to him first, her plump, smiling face pleasant and open and framed by honey-wheat hair that Bastian thought was quite beautiful.

"So, you're the boyfriend," she said, crossing her arms over an ample chest.

"Yep," Bastian said, a bit defensive. "I guess I'm the boyfriend."

Riley hugged her from behind and kissed her cheek. "Yes, Cheryl, he's the boyfriend."

Bastian wasn't sure he liked being called just 'the boyfriend'. He was about to actually introduce himself when the blond of the two guys in the living room nudged his way forward with a broad grin. "Hey, Bastian. Riley never shuts up about you. I'm Matt."

"Nice to meet you," he replied. He shook Matt's hand and tried to ignore the warm skin that pulsed against his. His eyes were drawn to Matt's wrist, and his stomach twisted. The hunger was worse. It almost never stopped nagging at him. He'd downed a water bottle of blood while Riley was prepping the snacks. It should have been enough. He would need to grab another shot from his backpack if he was going to get through tonight.

It then dawned on him he'd been holding Matt's hand, awkward silence in the room as Cheryl, Matt, and Riley watched him. He cleared his throat and released Matt's hand. He sighed with relief when Matt grinned at him and patted him on the shoulder.

"Damn, your hands are cold," Matt said. "Riley, don't you ever turn the heat on in here?"

A smile split Cheryl's face. "Cold hands, warm co—"

Riley reached out and slammed his hand over Cheryl's mouth. "*Thank* you, that's quite enough." He laughed and looked around the room as Cheryl pried his hand from her face. "Where'd Stephen disappear to?"

"Already grazing, I bet, assuming you have the usual food out," Cheryl said, craning her neck to look around the door frame of the kitchen.

"Get off my case, Cheryl!" Stephen's deep voice carried easily from the kitchen. "After two classes and my work shift, I'm fucking starving!"

Cheryl rolled her eyes. "You're always starving, you bottomless pit." She sat down on one of the chairs at the table and poked the Munchkin box. "Ooo, Munchkin. You're going easy on Bastian."

Riley pulled Bastian with him to the table. "I wouldn't call it going easy on him, but it's a lot of fun. I think you'll like it," he said, glancing at Bastian.

"What is it you do?" Matt asked as he sat beside Cheryl. "I mean, Riley says you're an art major or something?"

"Yeah," Bastian nodded, the tension in his shoulders loosening when Riley wrapped an arm around his waist, squeezing his hip encouragingly. "I thought I'd get into all sorts of art, but I just settled on a sculpting emphasis a couple months back."

Stephen sat at the table, his paper plate loaded with food. "You mean, like, pottery and shit?" He spoke with his mouth full, to which Cheryl scoffed. Bastian barely held back a laugh.

Riley sighed, the sound long and tortured. "Yes. Pottery that meant draping the entire room so nothing would get mud-spattered."

"Hey." Bastian elbowed Riley. "You're the one who said I could bring my homework here for a weekend."

"You freaked Zoe out so badly she hid under the bed all day." Riley elbowed him back, and if it weren't for Riley's bright smile, Bastian would have worried he hadn't been forgiven for that one.

"Poor cat," Matt snickered, grabbing a soda before opening the Munchkin box.

Bastian wet his lips, his stomach knotting again. This was a game they all knew, but which he'd never even heard of. He wanted to have fun, but he didn't want to be laughed at. "So, what is Munchkin?"

Cheryl began to shuffle one of the two decks. "It's cracked."

Riley nuzzled Bastian's throat. "Remember that conversation we had about Dungeons and Dragons? Well, if Dungeons and Dragons went on a drunken bender and had sex with an Uno deck, nine months later, you'd have Munchkin."

The group laughed, and Bastian laughed with them, though he didn't really understand what was funny. Yeah, the Dungeons and Dragons conversation had told him a lot, but he barely remembered any of it. Matt began to shuffle the second deck. "There are two decks?" Bastian asked.

Matt nodded. "The idea is to get from level one to level ten by fighting monsters. Along the way, you pick up treasure—gear and potions that can help you in the fights. It's very easy to pick up. Let's just start playing; you can learn as we go."

Stephen took a long drink of his soda, and then let out a loud belch. This earned him groans and a kick from Cheryl. Bastian watched as cards were dealt, counters were handed out, and, fuck, he was already lost.

Riley leaned over and smiled. "I'll help," he whispered.

Relief rushed through Bastian. "Good. I'll need it."

Riley stayed close and helped him rearrange his hand and put down the appropriate cards. It was worth the embarrassment of needing help just to have Riley's breath near his ear as he explained the basics.

"Aww, look at the cute couple," Matt cooed, batting his eyelashes at them.

"Just enough to ruin my appetite," Stephen said as he reached for another handful of tortilla chips and the bowl of salsa.

Bastian grinned broadly. "Then I guess it would bother you if I started doing this?" He turned Riley's chin toward him and kissed him in front of his friends. If they were such close friends of Riley's, well, then they probably saw this quite a lot in the past. Bastian let the world fall away, savoring this moment with Riley, even if they were watched.

Riley moaned as their tongues slid against one another, and Bastian felt one of the pale cheeks color under his hand. He chuckled, pulled back, and winked at Riley.

"Hot," Cheryl breathed.

Riley rolled his eyes and threw a cheese puff at her. "You're such a fag hag."

Cheryl laughed and fanned herself. "It's why I hang out with you and Matt, didn't you know?"

"I haven't had a beau to bring to game night in nearly a year," Matt muttered.

"Good point," Cheryl admitted with a smirk. "If you don't have someone by the end of the month, you're fired."

"It wasn't *his* fault," Stephen said. He raised a cupped hand to his mouth, as if that would make it possible for only Bastian to hear instead of the entire table. "Cheryl scared off the last one."

"I did not, asshole," Cheryl said, and the table jerked as another of her kicks made Stephen grimace. She smirked and took her turn, fighting the Web Troll monster and advancing another level. Bastian still wasn't sure how the whole monsters and levels and looting happened, but he was determined not to make a fool out of himself.

Bastian turned over a dungeon card, and while everyone else snickered, he just stared. "Wannabe Vampire?" he asked.

Riley laughed and nodded. "Yep. Because he was behind the door, you have to fight him or run away. You aren't a Cleric, so you can't do the booga booga thing."

"It's a bitch to draw monster cards before you have any sort of class or race," Cheryl said. "But... you're a Level Two with plus three thanks to your Chainsaw of Bloody Dismemberment, making you a Level Five. Which means, the Wannabe Vampire is kicking your ass."

Wannabe Vampire. His first time playing this game, and he drew the only vampire card in it. He ran his tongue over his fangs, self-conscious as everyone stared at him. "So, I'm losing?"

"Yep," Matt said. "However, you can ask for help. One of us can join with you and fight the vampire."

Stephen leered at him. "Helping isn't free, though."

Bastian laughed. It sounded high-pitched and odd to his ears. "What does it cost?"

"Depends on who you ask," Riley said. "Right now, only Matt or Cheryl can help you. Stephen and I aren't high enough in our levels to help."

Matt smiled, sweet and artificially innocent. "I'll help you."

The odd thought crossed Bastian's mind that he was beyond help, but then he blinked and looked back at the card game. "What would you want?"

"One of the treasures, I think," Matt said. "Since this is your first game, I'll go easy on you."

Riley gave him a nudge. "One treasure is very fair. You'll beat the vampire, go up a level, and still make out with two treasures yourself."

Bastian smiled at Riley, but Stephen's voice cut through the pleasant moment of looking into the turquoise eyes. "Whoa. You've got some teeth on you. Maybe *you're* the wannabe vampire."

It was meant to be a tease, but Bastian immediately stopped smiling, feeling blood rush to his cheeks. "Vampires aren't real," he muttered, trying to be as cool as possible. "I just happen to come from a family with sharp teeth."

"Besides," Riley purred, "they're quite nice when we're making out."

Bastian squeezed Riley's hand under the table, and though his lips did quirk upwards, the subdued smile didn't reach his eyes. "You like them when we're necking, too."

"Do go on," Cheryl encouraged with a grin.

"Or not," Stephen groaned, and Bastian exhaled slowly, glad the attention was at least momentarily off him and his teeth. "I came here to have fun, not watch Riley make out with his new boyfriend."

"But watching them *is* fun," Cheryl protested.

"I could make out with you so you won't feel left out," Matt offered, batting his eyelashes as he leaned over to rest his head on Stephen's shoulder.

Stephen instinctively hid his cards and laughed as he pushed Matt away. "No thanks, man. Besides, you think I'd give Cheryl the satisfaction? No way."

Bastian beat the Wannabe Vampire, Matt got his one treasure, he got two and leveled up, and the conversation flowed away from his teeth and vampires. It might no longer be the topic of conversation, but it never left his mind. Riley laughed with his friends. Cheryl kept making completely offensive comments and requests about their relationship. Stephen bemoaned the finishing of the salsa and chips. Bastian excused himself, needing to breathe, and went into the kitchen to fetch the bottomless pit more chips and dip.

"Bastian?"

Bastian turned around in the dim kitchen, coming almost face-to-face with Cheryl. "Hey, Cheryl." He tried to smile. "Just getting more snacks."

Cheryl didn't look so jovial and lecherous now, and Bastian shifted on his feet as she continued to stare at him. After a long, uncomfortable moment, she spoke. "I've known Riley since he was seven and I was six. We grew up together. Best friends. I knew he was gay before he did. I love him like a brother. It tore us both up when he went to Tennessee State and I came here. I'm the one who listened to him cry over the phone again and again every time Jake beat him up."

"Look, Cheryl–"

"I'm not *done*." Cheryl's eyes narrowed a little. "I picked him up in the middle of the night after he'd had Jake arrested. He spent all summer rearranging his life, picking up the pieces of his self-esteem. Now, Jake hasn't followed Riley here, and I hope the night in jail woke that asshole up, but Riley's been pretty gun shy about boyfriends. He hasn't dated much. So, when he popped up with your name and boyfriend attached to it, I was surprised. The fact that you've been mysterious and refusing to meet any of us has set off warning bells in my head."

Bastian gawked. He couldn't help it. This couldn't be the same woman who'd just ten minutes ago had asked Riley how far they'd gone in bed. It took him a moment to gather his wits, and then he was pissed. "You think I'm beating up on Riley?"

"Not physically, but from experience, I know you're hiding something." Cheryl stepped just a bit closer. "All I want you to know is, I'll kill you if you hurt him. He's been hurt enough for a lifetime. He doesn't need to be kicked around by you, too."

"I would *never* hurt Riley," Bastian hissed. "Never. He's important to me. Special. I have my reasons for waiting until now to meet his friends, but the point is, I've met you. You've met me. Who cares if it took a week or a whole goddamn year?"

Cheryl smiled at him. It was like a light switch with her. The shift from protective sister to perverse imp was startling. "I care, and I'm glad you do, too. It's all I needed to know."

"Damn right, I care," Bastian ground out, trying to calm down. His fist tightened on the bag of tortilla chips, making the paper bag crackle in the awkward silence that followed. Cheryl side-stepped him and grabbed a glass from the cupboard next to him. With her standing so close, he could hear her pulse like a soft drumbeat. Slow and steady, it was as if she hadn't just warned him to watch his ass. A jingle interrupted his concentration on Cheryl's pulse, and he looked down just as Zoe rounded the corner into the kitchen. Just the sight of the cat helped his pulse steady out, and he sighed. "Do you give death threats to everyone Riley introduces, or am I just special?"

Zoe meowed at him and rubbed against his leg. He set the chip bag aside, watching the way the crackle of the bag made Zoe's tail flick in expectation of treats. He picked her up and scratched her, smiling as her rumbling purr filled the quiet between him and Cheryl.

47

The silence lingered, and he frowned a little. Cheryl hadn't answered his question, and he looked over to see her staring at him again. His hand stopped scratching behind Zoe's ears. "What?" he asked while Zoe meowed her protest and nuzzled his hand.

"Oh, you're special all right," Cheryl chuckled, tapping the edge of her glass against Bastian's shoulder. "You make him happy. Let's keep it that way, hmm?"

Cheryl poured herself a glass of tea, giving him a final glance before stepping from the kitchen back into the living room. The guys grew louder for a moment, and then a shadow blocked the light from the doorway. Bastian looked up, and his heart skipped a beat. "Riley," he whispered.

Riley crossed over to him and slid his arms around his neck. "Bastian."

"Sorry it's taken a bit," Bastian murmured. "Cheryl wanted a few words."

Riley smiled and kissed Bastian lips softly. "She's like a sister. A nosy, perverted sister, but I love her anyway."

Bastian put Zoe down and hugged Riley. He buried his face against the warm, fragrant skin of Riley's neck. The blood pounded there, steady and strong, teasing at his senses. It was a tease he'd learned to ignore. He pressed several kisses to the thrumming pulse, earning a soft, breathy moan from Riley. "You're important to me."

Riley's arms tightened, holding him to his throat. His voice was thicker, deeper when he replied. "I know. You're important to me, too." Another moment passed, and then Riley said, "We should get back. I think Stephen is about ready to eat Cheryl."

Bastian straightened, a laugh easing the tension in him. "Oh, I'm sure she'd like that."

"I think so, too," Riley said, his eyes bright with happiness.

They grabbed several bags of chips, a tub of dip, and an extra large sub sandwich pre-sliced, everything carefully balanced as they left the kitchen for the brighter, warmer scene in the living room. Bastian handed off food, Cheryl made a crude comment about what they might have been doing in the kitchen, Matt lamented his own lack of date, and Stephen dove right into the sandwich. He sat down, surveying the group, how happy they were, and wondered if he really had a place in it all.

Riley pressed a cheese curl to his lips, and Bastian ate it, licking at his lover's fingers. The simple joy that positively radiated from Riley soothed all his worries. Even if he didn't have a place here with them, Riley would make one for him. Of that, Bastian was certain.

Chapter Five

"I want to suck you off," Riley whispered in his ear.

Riley's voice was rough, raspy as they moved against each other on the couch, and Bastian wasn't sure he'd heard right. He was distracted by how good Riley felt rubbing their groins together. This had become the status quo, and Bastian certainly hadn't pushed for more, but those words...

"What?" Bastian panted, trying to bring their lips together. He squeezed Riley's ass, pulling another moan from them both. "You want to what?"

Riley kissed from his ear to his lips, and then suckled on his tongue for a moment. Fuck. There was nothing sexier to Bastian than when Riley sucked at his tongue while all but riding him. At the moment, all Bastian wanted to do was continue their rocking, kiss Riley until they were both trembling on the cusp of climax, and then tumble over. His hands skated up the warm expanse of Riley's bare back, and he heard himself whimper when Riley pulled back to look him in the eyes.

"I want to suck you off." Riley's hands dropped down between their bodies, cupping him through the thick fabric of his jeans.

It was the first time in their nine month relationship that Riley had touched him like that, and Bastian closed his eyes and arched up into the touch. "Suck... me off?"

Riley leaned in, rubbing and squeezing at him. "Mm-hmm. Your cock... my mouth."

Bastian groaned. He'd had plenty of time to appreciate Riley's oral skills. Hell, he'd lost count of how many times he'd jerked off on his own to thoughts of Riley's mouth at his throat or cock. It was exactly what he'd been waiting for, the step he'd been yearning to take with Riley, but only when Riley was ready.

Another squeeze from Riley's hand forced the air from his lungs. "Yeah," he gasped. "God, yeah, I want that, too."

It wasn't that simple, though. It couldn't just be an effortless step forward. Ever since that first game night with Cheryl and the others, he'd promised himself that he wouldn't take this step without Riley knowing his secrets, knowing everything. It was only fair. Sex was such a big thing for Riley. Sex had meaning now that Bastian hadn't really thought to give it before. If they were going to finally take that step from dry humping to actual sex, Riley deserved to know him.

Know all of him, even the parts Bastian himself didn't understand or like.

As Riley rubbed at him and kissed him breathless, the last thing he wanted to do was stop the track they were on for a heart-to-heart, but Riley... If Riley reacted badly to what he was, he'd never be forgiven for springing it after they'd finally fucked, and he'd have Cheryl hunting him down within the hour. He couldn't fuck it up like that, and the thought of seeing Riley with a hurt, used expression on his face was enough for Bastian to pull back.

"Wait," he breathed, cupping Riley's face to keep their lips apart. He forced his eyes up to Riley's, and the need he could see reflected in them nearly stopped his already barely-beating heart. He licked his lips, not wanting to see uncertainty creep over Riley's flushed face. "Before we do this, I have to tell you something."

Riley blinked a couple of times, slowly, as if trying to decode what he was saying. "Is something wrong?"

"Maybe, maybe not." Bastian swallowed, gathered his courage. "I'm not like other guys."

A smile curved Riley's swollen lips. "I know." Riley tried to lean forward and kiss him again, but Bastian stopped him. "Bastian, what is it?"

The hot glow of need was beginning to fade in Riley's eyes, and Bastian could have kicked himself. He was in a no-win situation. It was going to fall apart no matter what he did, but if Riley kicked him to the curb, it would be because of the truth, not because he'd been used. "Remember that frat party I told you I went to in the spring freshman year?"

Riley nodded, sitting back on Bastian's knees and pulling his hand off Bastian's cock. "Yeah, I remember. You said it was your last one night stand. You were tired of going from guy to guy."

Bastian let out a slow breath. "That's a half-truth, Riley."

Confusion flitted over Riley's flushed face. "Half-truth?" he whispered.

"Don't look like that," Bastian said, kissing the corner of Riley's mouth. "There were things I... didn't know how to tell you. That last night was terrifying for me, Riley. It wasn't something I understood then. Hell, I don't even know if I understand it now. All I know is, that night changed my life."

"What happened?" Riley tried to shift off Bastian's lap, but Bastian stopped him. "What happened, Bastian?"

Bastian let go of Riley's hips, his heart racing as he tried to force the words out of his mouth. "I didn't even know the guy. He was hot, and that's all that mattered to me. I didn't care if he was smart or talented or kind. All I saw was dark eyes, beautiful skin, and a killer body." He laughed bitterly. "Killer body... I don't remember much after we took over one of the rooms. I don't think I want to remember." He held Riley's gaze with his own and whispered, "He hurt me, Riley."

"Did he rape you?" Riley's face filled with concern. "Did you change your mind or something?"

"You know, I almost wish it had been that." Bastian shook his head. "He bit me. He made me bleed."

The color drained from Riley's face. "Did you contract something? Is that what this is about? Did he give something to you?"

"Yeah," Bastian said. "He did, but it's not... it's not some STD I can go to the clinic and be treated for. I... I think he drank my blood. I think he killed me or something, because after that night, I wasn't really *alive* anymore." The words finally left him in a rush, fast and almost panicked. He didn't want to lose Riley, but, God, it was so wonderful to confide in someone! "I had his blood on my lips. He must have cut himself and made me drink his blood. I woke up and he was standing in the shadows getting dressed. He threw me my clothes and said, 'Things will be different now. Don't go out in the day unprotected, and you better find someone to munch on real soon.' Then, he left. He left me! I was covered in blood, freezing like my blood had been replaced with ice, and, Riley, I'd never been so thirsty... I got dressed, but stepping out into the sunlight made me sick, made my skin burn, and so I hid in the frat house until dusk."

"Bastian," Riley began, his brow furrowed.

"But I didn't go home. I was ravenous. I wanted the thirst to stop. I would have done *anything* to make it stop, but I didn't understand it. As I walked around the park, I looked at people. They weren't people to me, though, they were food. I knew in the pit of my stomach if I drank their blood, I'd feel better, but I didn't know what to do." Bastian closed his eyes. "I stumbled on some homeless guy under the footbridge. I bit him."

Riley jumped off his lap, terror having replaced lust. "You *what*?"

Bastian stood up. "I had to! Riley, please, please don't look at me like that. I didn't mean for it to happen. I couldn't help myself. I didn't get out of that thirsty haze until it was too late, until the hunger stopped and I realized I'd killed him." He broke off for a second, unable to continue without swallowing once. "I haven't done that sort of thing since! I drink pig or cow blood from the butcher. I survive without hurting *anyone*, I promise. Please... please, Riley..." he begged, reaching out for his lover. He needed to be reassured. The word that had been resounding in his head for months was only pushed back when Riley touched him, smiled at him, made him feel human instead of a monster.

"You're telling me you're—"

Bastian nodded, the weight of the world on his shoulders in that moment. "A vampire."

He'd said it.

The word had been spoken aloud. He was a vampire. A monster. It was real and true and out there now. He couldn't change it. No matter how much he wanted to, this was his life now. Blood and that cold feeling and the inhuman thing inside him that, even now, wanted to pin Riley to the wall and sink his teeth into the soft throat.

Riley shook his head. "Vampires aren't *real.*"

Bastian smiled ruefully. "I'm real."

Within the blink of an eye, the fear in Riley morphed into fury. "Why? Why did you wait to tell me? Why now?" he shouted.

"I wouldn't fuck you until you knew. I can't do that. Jake used you. He hurt you. I didn't want to be like him. I didn't want to be selfish. Sex is a big step for you—for *us*—and I didn't want this to come out after." Bastian held out his hands in surrender. "I wanted you to be able to choose knowing what I am. Riley, you matter so much–"

"I matter?" Riley stepped forward and gave Bastian's chest a sharp poke. "You've spent nine months lying to me, and I *matter*?"

"Of course you matter," Bastian insisted, rubbing instinctively at his chest. His throat felt tight, but he forced his voice to work. "I didn't lie; I just kept a secret because I was chickenshit. I had to be sure we meant something big to one another. I couldn't just tell anyone. They'd think I'm psycho!"

Riley shook his head. "You kept it from me this whole time. You don't do that with someone you care about. Not when it's this big." Bastian felt the weight of Riley's eyes as they raked over him. "I feel like I barely know you now."

Bastian grimaced and reached out for Riley, but Riley just stared at his outstretched hand, and he lowered it again, feeling like a damn fool. "You know me, Riley. It's still been me all these months. I'm still the guy who'd never seen *A Charlie Brown Christmas*. I'm still the guy who kissed you on New Year's and fell asleep on the couch with Zoe. I just... Now you know why I've been anti-social and have to bundle up so much outside. It's not just a disease... or maybe it is." He shifted on his feet and wrung his hands. Even though his heart beat quickly, it felt like ice pumping through his veins. "I don't really know what the hell it all is, but I'm cold all the time. I'm cold except when I'm close to you."

"You kept it from me," Riley murmured, averting his eyes. "A lie of omission is still a lie, Bastian. You know how important honesty is to me."

"I know, yes, I know, and maybe I did screw up keeping it from you for so long, but, please, try and see it from my point of view." Bastian took a step forward and was relieved when Riley didn't take a step back. "When we met, I was still changing. Those three weeks when I didn't call you? I lost my canine teeth and had to watch as *fangs* grew in. I was trying to figure out how much blood was enough to keep from being overwhelmed around you. When we met, I was lost." He smiled and took the chance to reach out again. Riley didn't flinch or bat his hand away, so he cupped Riley's cheek. "I'm not anymore. I kept it from you because I was afraid. I'm telling you now because..."

Riley licked his lips, and Bastian could feel his pulse flutter rapidly under his fingers. "Because?"

"Because I love you."

Surprise lit Riley's eyes. "You love me?"

"I have for a while; I just didn't know if you would believe me if I said it." Bastian tilted his head, his thumb tracing Riley's cheekbone. "You're everything I never even knew to look for in a guy. You're smart, kind, care about family, have goals but can be spontaneous, too. You've always seen me for me, even if you didn't know this part, and you cared enough to try to help. You're someone I trust, love being around, and don't want to lose."

His chest felt tight with the truth of that last statement. Losing Riley might not kill him, but it'd be a deep cut, one he didn't think would heal for a long time. "Please, Riley. Maybe I should have told you sooner, but I'm telling you now. You've got to believe me when I say I don't want to hurt you."

"You hurt me by lying," Riley pointed out. There was less fire in his voice, though, and Bastian could feel the tension easing out of Riley's face.

"I know," Bastian murmured, "and I'm sorry. I can't promise I'll never hurt you. I can't promise there won't be misunderstandings or drama, but if you keep me around, I can at least promise I'll be honest from now on."

Riley stared at him for a long time. "So. You're a vampire."

Bastian nodded once. "Yeah."

"But, you don't eat people. Or animals." Riley narrowed his eyes. "If you ever think to eat Zoe, I'll—"

"I *won't* eat Zoe." Bastian laughed softly. "I don't *eat* anyone. I go to a butcher. It's blood that would otherwise go to waste, but it keeps me sane."

Riley shuffled closer. "Don't lie to me again. Don't keep things from me. I'm a big boy. I can deal with... vampires."

A weight eased from Bastian's shoulders, and he opened his arms to Riley. He was shorter than Riley, but he didn't care when the distance between them closed. He wrapped his arms around Riley's waist and rested his cheek and ear against Riley's chest. The heat of being close and the sound of Riley's heartbeat pulled a pleased sigh from him. When Riley's arms circled his shoulders, he thought he'd die of relief. Riley wasn't pissed off anymore. That was a big step forward, but a question still burned in his mind. "Does this mean I get to stay?"

Riley nodded, his cheek pressed against Bastian's head. "Yeah, and I can think of a few ways you can make it all up to me."

Bastian forced himself back to look up at Riley. "Is that a 'litter box duty for a month' tone or a 'be my love slave' tone?"

Riley snorted. "Which would you prefer?"

Bastian smiled. "Definitely the second one."

"Then it's the litter box for you," Riley said.

"I figured. Do you... have any questions?"

Riley pulled back a little and looked down at him. "I have a lot of them, but I think I need to process all of this. Promise me I'll get to have my moment of freak out when the shock wears off?"

"You're going to put this in a box and shelve it in your mind?"

A smile twitched at Riley's lips. "Yeah, I am."

Bastian craned his neck, pressing a brief, soft kiss to Riley's lips. "Promise. As long as that freak out doesn't involve pushing me out into the sunlight shirtless, we're good. I'll answer any questions you have, too."

"All right." Riley slid his hands down Bastian's neck and over his chest. He leaned down and brushed his lips over Bastian's throat. "Then I'm going to pretend, just for tonight, that this conversation didn't happen." He nipped, and Bastian groaned, lust igniting in him with frightening intensity. "You're just a normal guy, my boyfriend, and we're going to make love." A scrape of teeth, and Bastian's knees nearly buckled. "Tomorrow, I'll go crazy, yell, ask questions, and be scared, but tonight... tonight it's us, the bed, and a package of condoms."

Bastian scratched lightly down Riley's back and squeezed Riley's ass. When the anger had erupted, Bastian hadn't dared to hope for this chance. Now that it was offered again, he grabbed it with both hands. "You want me inside," he panted. "You've wanted me inside for a long time, haven't you?"

"Yes," Riley moaned against his throat, every breath a soft tease that made Bastian ache with need.

"Tonight, you're mine." Bastian trailed one hand Riley's body, his fingers circling and rolling one nipple. Riley gasped and pulled back from his neck as a shudder moved through his body. Riley was stunning, beautiful, and Bastian thanked his lucky stars for this second chance. He leaned forward and kissed up the line of Riley's neck from collarbone to ear. The strong, fast pulse beneath his lips called to that sixth sense of his, a sweet reminder of Riley's life. It was something to cherish, and he reverently nuzzled and suckled the skin. He wanted Riley to know he could be close without hurting him, that being a vampire didn't change how much he cared. "You're mine, and I'm yours."

"Bedroom," Riley moaned, pressing his chest into Bastian's fingers.

Bastian shuffled them toward the bedroom, nearly sending them both to the floor when they tripped over their discarded shoes. In the relative safety of the hallway, he finally pulled Riley into a deep kiss, pausing for a minute to press him against the wall. He couldn't help himself. The need to taste Riley and drown in the sensation of him sent sparks tingling down his spine.

Riley tugged at the fastening of his jeans, slid down the zipper, and shoved his hand in. As they devoured each other, Riley's hand closed around him, stroked him, and Bastian swore he'd never felt anything so intense. He groaned and pushed Riley tighter to the wall. Riley began to suck his tongue again, and Bastian didn't want to wait anymore. Bastian yanked Riley the rest of the way into the bedroom, his eyes taking in the hard bulge in Riley jeans and the flushed, hungry expression on his face.

"I want to suck you off," Riley said, echoing his earlier request. He flicked his wrist, undoing the button and zipper on his jeans. Riley shoved them down, and Bastian watched as he saw his first glimpse of Riley naked. "We can do anything else after, but I want that first."

"No problem," Bastian whispered, unable to truly speak while he stared. His heart pounded in his chest, and he licked his lips as his eyes traveled over Riley.

"Something wrong?" Riley asked, a knowing smile on his lips. He ran his own fingers over a nipple and pinched it lightly with a hum of pleasure. It was just the tease Bastian needed to jar him back into action.

"You're fucking perfect," Bastian said and took Riley's mouth with his once more. He wanted to touch every inch of Riley, especially the areas that had stayed off limits to his hands before tonight. He followed the curve of

Riley's back to his ass and took in the smooth, hot skin before bringing one hand forward to stroke Riley's long, slender cock. It had never been this good through their jeans. Even his light grip pulled a needy moan from Riley. Bastian knew he could jack Riley off in no time, but he didn't want it all to end that fast.

Bastian broke the kiss as he stepped back. His breath was short and quick as he pushed his own jeans and underwear impatiently to the floor. It wasn't often he felt overheated, but Riley made his blood rush and his skin burn to be touched. As soon as he was naked, he pulled Riley flush against his body and tumbled to the bed, laughing softly with Riley. "Perfect," he insisted, his hands stroking from Riley's shoulders down to his ass.

"Not quite." Riley squirmed down his body, glanced up at him, and then drew his tongue up from Bastian's balls to the tip of his cock.

"Oh, fucking hell," Bastian said as he spread his legs wider. "You are so sexy when you do that."

Riley did it again and again, those burning blue-green eyes always canted up to look at him. Bastian thought he would go crazy. This wasn't sucking him off. This was testing his limits of patience. He reached down and threaded his fingers through Riley's soft, copper hair and urged him up to the head of his cock. That was all it took. In an instant, his entire length was engulfed in the most luxurious heat. He'd been swallowed whole, and his mind reeled at the pleasure that shot through him.

Bastian's hips tensed, and he fought not to buck up deeper into Riley's throat when it tightened rhythmically around him. He cried out, fisting his hand in Riley's hair. It was too much. If Riley kept that up, he was going to come.

Just when he was about to warn Riley between harsh moans, Riley pulled back to gasp in a breath.

"You taste good," Riley panted, giving them both a brief respite before sucking the tip of Bastian's cock back between his lips.

"You, too. I mean–ah!" Bastian bucked uncontrollably, but Riley moved fluidly with him. All the hints at what Riley could do with his mouth through those deep kisses all these months were nothing compared to his lover's talent. Another swipe of that tongue into his slit, and all words fled from his mind. He watched as Riley licked and stroked him, bobbing slowly up and down. His eyelids became heavier, but he forced them to stay open. He wouldn't look away. He wouldn't miss a moment. Watching made it so much more real, and locking eyes with Riley left him gasping.

Their pulses thundered in his ears. The sound of rushing blood and pleasure. It surrounded him like a warm embrace, made his throat ache with sudden thirst. Riley pushed him higher and higher, but just when he thought he would come, Riley pulled back. "Riley!" he cried out, finally squirming, his hips straining upward for the touch that would send him over the edge.

Their eyes locked, and time stood still for an instant. Bastian could have sworn there was an order there in those eyes, but it was wrapped up in too many layers of emotion that he couldn't decipher through the haze of his own need. His eyes remained on Riley's as heat enveloped his cock again, and he watched as Riley made a firm stroke of mouth and fist. And then another. His breath caught in his throat. The third stroke made his toes curl as he shouted, coming over Riley's tongue.

Riley swallowed every drop, sucking at him until it became almost painful. Bastian eased Riley off him, and then pulled Riley up to lay atop him. He kissed the sweet, slick lips as he tried to catch his breath. His body still pounded with the lingering pleasure. "Fuck, Riley," he said with a grin.

"Good?" Riley thrust against him, small movements of restless need.

Bastian licked across Riley's lower lip. "Good? Riley, that was..." He didn't have any word other than 'perfect', and he'd said that two or three times already. "What do you want? I can't fuck you. I need at least half an hour to recover, but," he murmured, dipping the tip of his tongue between Riley's parted lips, "I can do anything else you want."

Riley shifted against him, moaning softly as they kissed. "This," he breathed. "You kissing me, touching me, until I come."

Bastian ran his hands from Riley's arms down to his ass and upper thighs. "Like this?" he teased, making another long stroke with his palms. "Or maybe something more like this," he suggested with a light scratch to Riley's backside while he nipped Riley's lower lip.

Riley moaned, the sound almost desperate. "I don't care," he said, his eyes heavy-lidded. "Just... touch me."

There was something so needy in those word, in the tone that made Bastian's ears prick. Jake, Bastian fully realized, had done deep, lasting damage. One day, he'd ask what that damage was, but for now, he'd give Riley everything he could.

Bastian rolled them onto their sides and kissed Riley sweetly, gently. His hand skirted Riley's hip, dipped between their bodies. With a soft moan, he took Riley in hand again. Bastian stroked up and down, his tongue sliding against Riley's. He swiped his thumb over the wet, sticky tip, drank in the quiet sounds Riley gifted him with. Bastian wanted to see Riley undone, writhing and screaming, but Riley was subdued.

"Let me hear you," Bastian whispered against Riley's ear. "You can let it all out."

He squeezed his hand around Riley and nipped his throat, and Riley let a rasping cry. It moved through him and made his heart leap in his chest. He kissed down Riley's chest, captured a nipple, and sucked. Riley jerked against him, a loud, full-throated cry filling the room. Bastian smiled against Riley's chest, Riley's hand in his hair, and sucked, tugged, and laved at the nipple. He tormented it, wringing cry after cry out of Riley, and his hand move swiftly over Riley's straining cock.

Every cry and moan, every twitch and shift of Riley against him, hinted at emotions deep inside Riley that Bastian longed to know. Hurts he wanted to heal. Needs he wanted to satisfy. Jake had done nothing but take, but Bastian wanted to give. He gave with each stroke of his hand and kiss of his lips. The sounds of Riley's pleasure echoed off the walls, accompanied by the rapid pulse that drummed against his palm and lips. Riley's trembling hands tightened at his shoulder and in his hair, and he pumped Riley as fast as he could. Pulling off Riley's throbbing nipple, he quickly kissed his way to the other and breathed, "You can let go. Let go, Riley."

Riley gasped and stilled against him for an instant, and then there was that first hot splash against Bastian's fingers and stomach. He shivered and latched onto Riley's untouched nipple, making Riley scream as he bucked. The pleasure in that sound was more than worth the stinging of his scalp where Riley pulled at his hair. His heart ached in his chest when the scream tapered off into a sob.

He softened his touches and kissed his way back up to Riley's mouth, shifting so his free hand could cup Riley's flushed face and brush away stray hairs from his eyes. "You okay?"

Riley shivered, nodded, and clung to him. "Yeah, I am, just..." He let out a long, shaky breath. "It felt amazing."

Bastian smiled and kissed Riley again. "Good."

Riley sighed, the tension in his body easing with the release of that breath. "Thank you for telling me," he whispered.

Bastian wrapped his arms around Riley and pulled him closer. "You're welcome. I'd hoped I could trust you. Just didn't want to ruin what we had."

"You haven't," Riley murmured, and the reassurance made Bastian kiss him all over again.

"Everything'll be all right. It's only gonna get better." There was still that processing and freak out for them to deal with in the morning, but right now, that didn't matter. All that mattered to Bastian was the warmth of Riley's weight against him, the scent of sex, and the hope he had for them both. "I promise, it'll only get better," he whispered as Riley's breathing deepened with oncoming sleep.

Riley

Chapter Six

Riley sat on the bed and watched Bastian hang up his clothes in the space he'd made for him. Things had progressed rapidly once they'd gone to bed with each other. Riley supposed the last ten months had been leading to this moment. Bastian had been practically a daily aspect of his life for the last month. After they'd slept together, Bastian hadn't really gone back to his dorm room. Zoe had adjusted, his friends had called him crazy, and then... then hc'd askcd Bastian to movc in.

Bastian threw a grin his way. "Do I get a drawer?"

"You get the bottom three," Riley said, unable to keep from smiling in return. "I'm generous, remember?"

"I remember." Bastian started to load in his boxers and socks, and Riley continued to watch him.

Bastian had moved in. Riley had been careful this time. He'd dated Bastian. He'd made Bastian earn his trust. Of course, that whole vampire thing—which he still wasn't so sure about—had dented the trust a bit, but he'd bounced back. Bastian loved him, after all, and... well... he loved Bastian. Riley didn't want to end things with him. He wanted to see many more years with Bastian, and if the legends were right, they'd have them in spades.

"I'm still paying part of the rent, though," Bastian insisted as he moved on to the second drawer and unloaded his casual shirts from his trash bag full of clothes. "Just 'cause I'm your live-in boyfriend now doesn't mean I should get a free ride. I'm already getting in your way with my painting stuff."

That had been a three-day argument. Riley hadn't wanted Bastian to contribute any money but to the food budget, but Bastian had wanted to go fifty-fifty. Bastian had won. "I don't use the second bedroom for much. It's small, but it's yours. It'll be perfect once we set it up."

Bastian turned to face him, his eyes alight with pleasure. "And this room?"

Warmth unfurled in Riley, made his pulse flutter in his throat. Just a look, and he was ready to drop to his knees and worship Bastian. "This room is *our* room."

Bastian closed his eyes and sighed happily, leaning his head against the open drawer for a moment. When the hazel eyes opened, they darted to the window, and then back to Riley. "You sure you won't mind giving up mornings with the sun streaming onto the bed?"

Having Bastian around meant keeping all of the windows carefully covered during the day. Oh, there was still light through the curtains, but it was a muted kind of light that allowed Bastian to walk around in his boxers. Walking about in boxers meant Riley could easily indulge in his personal pursuit to blow Bastian in every room of the apartment, and then they could work on the fucking. He smiled, trying to reassure Bastian. "I don't mind. Having the curtains up feels like we live in twilight. I like it."

"You like it?" Bastian chuckled, putting the last of his shirts in the drawer and nudging it closed. Rounding the trash bag, Bastian started crawling toward him. Even in the half-light, Riley could see that seductive glint to Bastian's eyes. When Bastian spoke again, his voice had lowered to a purr that sent a shiver of pleasure through him. "You like the light soft so it leaves shadows that play along the curves and lines of our bodies?"

Riley's mouth was dry. "Yes." Was his voice really that breathy? No, it couldn't be. But he was breathing fast, bordering on hyperventilating as his eyes followed Bastian. Bastian moved with grace. A predator's sensuality, Riley supposed. He hadn't seen it before, but now he knew what to look for. Now he knew what made him achingly hard.

Bastian's eyes raked over him. It was as arousing as any touch Bastian had bestowed upon him. Bastian crawled right up to his knees and parted them to kneel in front of his groin. Even fully dressed, Riley felt completely exposed, his erection a prominent bulge in his jeans. Bastian rubbed up and down his thighs, his hands always stopping short of his groin in a way that soon had Riley panting softly. "I should paint you," Bastian murmured, leaning forward to rub his cheek against Riley's cock.

Riley moaned. "Paint me?"

"Mm-hmm," Bastian said. "Get you hard and pose you. I'd keep you in place, keep you hard for hours so I could paint the light playing over your body."

Riley swallowed against the desert that had taken up residence in his throat. "That... isn't medically advisable."

"Ah, but you knew that before you invited me to live here." Bastian smiled up at him. "I think you *want* to be driven crazy. I think you need someone to make you feel like every inch of you is beautiful." Bastian scratched a single nail firmly down the length of him through his jeans, and he moaned, heat rising in his cheeks.

"You think so?"

"I do." Bastian reached up and slid the button of his fly open. "I think you need me to offer you release in ways you've only dreamed about."

Riley closed his eyes for a moment, and the sound of the zipper on his jeans opening was deafening to his ears. "Yes... yes, I do," he admitted on an exhale.

"No strings attached," Bastian murmured as he pulled Riley's cock free. One long lick from base to tip, and Riley's toes were already curling. "No expectations except to feel everything that's good. No apologies. What's in your dreams, Riley?"

"My dreams?" Riley moaned, watching the head of his cock disappear between Bastian's lips.

Bastian hummed and nodded, refusing to part with his cock. The slickness of Bastian's tongue swirled over him, and sharp teeth teased over the head. Bastian was always careful, but that edge of danger made his heart skip a beat and a thrill run down his spine. His dreams? His dreams had always seemed so simple to him. Safety. Security. He dreamed of not being afraid, and he shuddered, spreading his legs wider.

"I dream about being a vet."

Bastian let his cock slip from his lips with an audible pop. "Not that sort of dream." Riley watched Bastian creep up his body, unbuttoning his shirt and pushing it from his shoulders. "Late at night, when you were alone, what did you dream about?"

Riley cried out the moment Bastian's lips latched onto his nipple. He was so sensitive, and when Bastian added the touch of his hand on his cock, Riley wasn't sure he could even talk. He didn't even think he wanted to.

Talking could wait. Right now, he knew what he wanted. "Fuck me," he groaned. "Shut up and fuck me, please, Bastian."

Bastian chuckled against his chest. "I'll get an answer eventually," he warned, but Riley was relieved when Bastian tapped his hips. He lifted them and bit his lip with excitement as Bastian peeled his jeans and boxers off his legs.

Completely naked on the bed while Bastian was still fully clothed, Riley shifted restlessly before he reached out to help with Bastian's clothes. "I want to feel you."

"My mouth wasn't good enough?" Bastian was only teasing, and it made Riley laugh softly. Bastian pulled his t-shirt up over his head and pushed down his pants.

Riley didn't bother with an actual answer to the question. His mouth was busy kissing up Bastian's chest to his neck. He sucked over the pulse. Bastian moaned loudly, and the sound sent a thrill through Riley. It hadn't taken him long to learn that Bastian's neck was his weakest point, and Riley never missed a chance to exploit it.

He pulled Bastian down over him, his hands smoothing down pale, cool skin while his mouth worried a bright bruise on Bastian's throat. The bruise wouldn't last, as they'd quickly discovered, but it always gave Riley an excuse to start the day off between them with a hickey. Riley arched against Bastian, his body so hot against the coolness of Bastian's, and he groaned, parting his legs to let Bastian settle between his. It wasn't going to be drawn out lovemaking, but that wasn't what Riley wanted. What he wanted was to be fucked into the mattress. This was the day Bastian moved in, became as permanent a fixture in his life as anyone could be, and Riley wanted to remember it vividly.

Riley broke away from Bastian's throat, pleased to
see the bright red spot with a center of darkening purple.
He had little time to gloat, though, as Bastian immediately
claimed his lips in a searing kiss. Everything moved quickly.
He'd been so patient, tentative, waiting to see if Bastian
would hit him, yell at him, cheat on him, but Bastian hadn't.
All the heavy petting and dry humping, the movie nights
and gaming with his friends, it had led to this. One night of
sex, and he'd asked Bastian to move in with him. One
month of preparations, and now Bastian was about to fuck
him on *their* bed, in *their* apartment, with *their* condoms.

Bastian reached over him and rummaged in the top
nightstand drawer for the condoms and Astroglide. How he
managed to do that and circle his hips at the same time,
Riley didn't know, but it stretched Bastian's neck out
appealingly. He couldn't resist teasing his mark all over
again, which caused Bastian's hips to jerk forward.

"Fuck," Bastian groaned, shoving the drawer shut
and all but collapsing atop Riley for a moment.

Riley scraped his teeth over the bruise and drew a
line down Bastian's spine with his fingertips. "That's the
idea."

Bastian choked out a laugh between moans. Riley
heard the top of the lube bottle snap open, and a second
later, Bastian's hand pushed its way between their bodies.
The slick fingers massaged at him for a moment, and his
breath hitched in his throat as two slid inside. Riley's head
lolled back against the bed as he arched his hips. Bastian's
mouth found his throat, and the world was painted in red
behind Riley's eyelids. His mind was bent on being fucked,
and while Bastian dithered, sucking at his throat while

thrusting his fingers in and out, impatience reared up in him.

Riley bucked up and threw his weight. The action forced Bastian's fingers from him, but it allowed him to get on top. He straddled Bastian's hips and grinned. Riley plucked at Bastian's nipples, and the surprise bled from Bastian's face, replaced with a lusty smile.

"Impatient much?" Bastian asked.

Riley snatched a condom from the nightstand. "When someone asks to be fucked, it would be wise of you to oblige."

"I was getting there!"

Riley laughed as he slid the condom down Bastian's cock. "I'd rather be there already."

Bastian stroked quickly over the condom, using the rest of the lube from his hand with a smirk. "You on top's sexier anyway," he reasoned, pulling Riley forward and positioning them.

Just as Riley began sitting down, Bastian thrust up to meet him, taking him in one, sure movement. Pleasure and pain shot through him, forcing the air from his lungs in a rough cry. He barely heard Bastian's echoing shout, his focus narrowing to where their bodies joined. His muscles protested for a moment, making Bastian feel even thicker, stretching him wide. The pain lasted only a few heartbeats, and then it dimmed, faded into the background, and Riley rocked against Bastian.

"Ah!" Those small, initial movements were the best, in Riley's opinion. Smooth and slippery, a soft rasp against nerves that made his cock twitch. Bastian's fingers found his nipples again, and pleasure flooded him. His vision cleared after a moment, and his heart thundered in his chest when he saw the hunger in Bastian's eyes. Jake had never looked at him like that, and the sex had never been this good. It was exactly what he'd wanted, and his cock ached between his legs as he began to rise and fall on Bastian.

Bastian met his pace, gave him a little time to adjust before urging him faster with a deep thrust. A sharp tug at his nipples scattered his thoughts and made him falter as he arched with a gasp. "So fucking hot," Bastian growled.

Riley rode Bastian fast, hard, balanced carefully against his pale, broad chest. Bastian's fingers were unrelenting at his nipples, driving him crazy. His toes curled as the singular thought of orgasm filled his head. He wanted to feel Bastian come inside him. He wanted to sit back, full of Bastian, and shout his release to the ceiling. It was wild and free. It was for him and no one else. Riley took what he wanted, even as he gave of himself, and he knew he was in safe hands.

He slammed down on Bastian again and again, opening his eyes to watch the pleasure fill Bastian's beautiful face. Hazel eyes seemed to burn into him, see to the very core of him, and Riley shivered violently, squeezing Bastian with his inner muscles. On one side was his life without Jake, alone and scarred, licking his wounds while laughing with his friends, and on the other side was his life with Bastian. Here, he was bathed in warmth, taken care of without being coddled. What scars he had were revered, and what wounds still needed healing were carefully tended to.

Riley closed his eyes, bounced on Bastian's lap, Bastian's cries and grunts loud in his ears. They soared higher, and Riley's thighs began to burn, but he pushed on as Bastian's body began to twitch and his sounds became more desperate. Riley's focus became that moment, that beautiful, fulfilling moment when Bastian was utterly his. A few minutes later, pushed to his own physical limits, Riley was rewarded. Bastian shouted, hands dropping from his chest to grasp his hips almost painfully. Bastian held tightly to him, jerking, making small, rocking motions as he came. Satisfaction filled Riley, even if the condom kept Bastian's seed from him.

Bastian's chest moved beneath his hands, heaving in deep breaths. It was a few seconds before Bastian's eyes fluttered open again, but the sated smile that spread over Bastian's face was worth the wait. Riley shifted, rocking again the instant Bastian's grip loosened. His thighs burned, protested every movement, and he moaned, his nails digging in at Bastian's chest.

"Kiss me," Bastian panted, reaching up and pulling Riley down. It changed the angle of his body, made it even more difficult for him to thrust himself down, but Bastian took over, claiming his mouth and thrusting with surprising force. His cries were devoured as Bastian gave him everything he needed. A hand closed around his cock and pumped furiously.

The slapping of their bodies together as Bastian overwhelmed his senses seemed to mirror the rhythm of his heart. Fast, hard, loud, and the pressure of Bastian's hand around his cock stole every thought from him. He writhed, hypersensitive, as he danced on that razor edge of climax, pain and pleasure colliding in him. Riley's breath hitched, his whole body stiff, and then it slammed into him. He sat back on Bastian, taking him completely inside once more, and screamed, his nails raking down Bastian's chest. It was fire in his blood, his whole body shaking with the force of his release as he came over Bastian's fist.

After a moment, he fell forward again, gasping, rubbing himself against Bastian's hand and stomach. Riley drew out the pleasure, made it last, savored every moment as he burned inside his own skin. The past on one side, the future on the other, and he gladly stepped forward.

When his breathing evened out, his ear pressed to Bastian's chest as Bastian stroked his hand up and down his back, Riley managed to force words past his parched lips. "I dream of you," he croaked. "I think I've always dreamed of you."

Riley awoke to an empty bed, and he grumbled, tossing about for a couple minutes before forcing himself to look at the clock. He frowned. It was nearly half past ten. That couldn't be right. He never slept in that late. He eyed the empty sheets next to him. If Bastian was out of bed, though, he had to assume the clock was right. With the windows covered in the bedroom, the daylight hours all seemed to blur together.

He rolled out of bed and headed straight for the shower. His morning routine took hold, and by the time he was out of the steamy bathroom, the scent of something baking drew his attention. He threw on a robe and peeked down the hallway. Zoe jingled down the hall and meowed at him, licking her chops. Bastian must have either fed her or slipped her a treat. Either way, the thought made him smile as he picked her up and padded to the kitchen.

His jaw dropped as he took in the disheveled state of the kitchen. Baking ingredients were everywhere, scattered over the counters with mixing bowls, egg shells, and a half-empty bag of frozen blueberries. In the middle of the kitchen, his back to the doorway, was Bastian in his pajama bottoms and an apron. Riley wasn't sure if he should be amused or horrified. "Oh, God..."

Bastian jumped at the sound of his voice and turned. "Riley! Fuck! Don't scare me like that."

"What have you done to my kitchen?" Zoe struggled in Riley's arms when he raised his voice, so he set her down before running his fingers through his damp hair, his eyes scanning the mess again.

Bastian's face grew pink, a sure sign that he'd had a good amount of blood to drink already. "Yeah, um... sorry. I'll clean it all up. Promise. It's just been a while since I've done something like this, and I got carried away. Go ahead and sit down. I'll have everything ready in a minute."

Riley gawked for a moment before sitting at the small kitchen table. Bastian had made breakfast for him? It was almost too cliché, too domestic. A smile slowly spread across his lips despite it all, and he watched Bastian grab a couple muffins from the cooling rack and dish out the eggs and sausage. Bastian set down the steaming plates with a grin. "I'd have done this when I first moved in, but you have a way of distracting me in the morning."

Now it was Riley's turn to flush. "I didn't know you cooked." Most nights when Bastian had shared a meal with him, he'd cooked. Those that he didn't, they ordered out. "It looks amazing," he said, and then his stomach made an audible gurgle. He laughed and picked up his fork. "And it's perfect timing, too."

Bastian sat with him, and they ate in uncomfortable— for Riley, at least—silence. It was somewhat awkward sharing space with someone else again, but he was actually starting to look forward to coming back from work or class knowing someone other than his cat was waiting for him. He glanced up at Bastian and offered a smile. Damn, the blueberry muffins were delicious.

"Exams are coming up," Bastian said.

Riley nodded. "I'll be studying a lot with Stephen. He's in three of my classes. He usually comes over here every day when we're gearing up for finals. Midterms, it's every other day, but finals..." Finals were hellish for everyone, and the more studying they could do, the better.

"That's cool by me," Bastian said between bites of egg. "I have a lithography project that's a pain in my ass, and that has to be done on campus, but the rest of my stuff I can do here. I... can set up my pottery wheel in the other room if you want, so I won't have to drape everything and Zoe won't freak. I have a couple things to throw and a sculpture and a painting to finish. I try to pace myself during the semester, but final projects always kick my ass."

"The spare room is all yours." Riley sipped his orange juice. "Just make sure you still cover everything because I would like to get my deposit back if we move."

Bastian gave him a wink. "Of course. I wouldn't ruin your apartment."

"*Our* apartment," Riley corrected. He was trying to get used to saying it himself.

"Our apartment," Bastian echoed. Again, silence fell between them, comfortable and easy this time, while they ate. It was Bastian who broke it, and Riley was not expecting the question that came out of his boyfriend's mouth. "How did you meet Jake?"

Riley choked on his eggs. "What?"

"You never really talked about him much, and I didn't think it was my business before, but we're, like..." Bastian trailed off, gesturing to the messy kitchen with his fork.

"Cohabitating?" Riley supplied, coughing between gulps of water.

"Exactly," Bastian nodded but paused. "You okay? I didn't mean to kill you with shock."

"I just wasn't expecting that question." But he should have, Riley realized. "I met him at a party."

"What party?"

Riley put his fork down. This was happening whether he wanted it to or not. Jake was the elephant in the room, looming even larger than Bastian's vampirism. "It was a mutual friend's twentieth birthday party. Jake looked gorgeous, said all the right things, and I fell for it hook, line, and sinker. Why did you go upstairs with that guy? Didn't you get the creeps from him or something?" Turnabout was fair play, and if they were going to talk about his demons, they would also talk about Bastian's.

"Did you get the creeps from me?" Bastian asked.

"No."

"Then no, I didn't get the creeps from him. He was hot, heavy-handed, and just what I wanted that night."

Riley frowned. "You liked fucking around?"

"It was just kind of part of the whole partying gig. Everybody at home knows I'm gay, but if I brought home some boyfriend back in high school, they'd have had a conniption fit." Bastian fiddled with his silverware. "I just sort of learned to keep things casual, so once I got to college, I went a bit wild."

"Sounds like it was more than 'a bit wild'."

"All right. So I fucked around a lot," Bastian admitted. "That doesn't mean I didn't want something like what we have. When that one-nighter happened, everything changed. It wasn't worth it to take a chance on some douche anymore just for a good fuck."

"But you didn't even know he was a douche when you went with him."

"I know," Bastian groaned. "That's what was so disturbing about it. He looked normal, acted normal, fucked like a wet dream, and I thought it was all good until he bit me. There weren't any little red flags or alarm bells. There wasn't shit to tell me I had to be careful around him. If I couldn't tell with him, how could I tell with anyone?"

Riley shook his head. "But he'd already done the worst he could. What else could someone have done that he hadn't?"

Bastian sighed. "I was afraid, all right? I was afraid I'd be the monster he'd been next time I just hopped into bed with someone. The way the hunger makes me feel? I didn't want to hurt or kill someone. But you, you found out Jake was an asshole."

"Yes." Riley shifted, uncomfortable with the turn of conversation. Jake was that dark spot, that time he wanted to forget but just couldn't. If it wasn't Cheryl checking to make sure he was all right, it was his sister asking if his new boyfriend was a big a prick as his last. Or, it was his own nightmares waking him in the middle of the night with a scream in his throat. It was tiring. "But only after we moved in together."

"How long did you wait before that happened?"

Riley kept his mouth shut. He didn't want to admit he'd made Bastian pay for Jake's mistakes. Bastian nudged

Riley with his foot under the table. Riley huffed and stood up, leaving his breakfast behind. "I don't want to talk about this."

"We have to sometime," Bastian sighed, standing and crossing his arms. "I don't like talking about how I was turned into a vampire, but it has to happen. I'd rather we talk now than wait another year and let things get stickier when we're not looking."

Riley stopped in the doorway. "Why does it matter? Jake's gone. In the past." Where Riley wanted Jake to stay.

"Because there are times when I'd swear you're waiting for me to hit you." Bastian took a step toward him. "You're still living in his shadow, and you shouldn't have to."

"And you're still denying what you are, even after a year," he shot back.

Bastian glared at him. "Don't change the subject. When did you move in with Jake?"

"About three weeks after I met him!" Riley flushed with shame. He'd been so stupid. Cheryl had warned him. When he'd called to tell her, gush about how exciting it was and what a great guy he'd found in Jake, Cheryl had told him he couldn't know that. Not for sure, and not in a matter of weeks. "He wasn't living on campus, and I was. He thought it would help me financially if I moved in with him. I was working all the time at a shit job and my grades were slipping. Jake had a great place, he'd treated me wonderfully, and I liked him. I thought, hell, he could be The One."

"But he wasn't."

Riley lifted his chin. He may have fucked up, but he'd learned from it. He'd survived. "No, he wasn't." That bruised place inside, the place that hadn't healed even when he'd left Jake, ached now. He didn't want to hurt. Riley was tired of being hurt by a memory. But, the memory *did* hurt. The memory made his heart twist, his throat tighten, and his eyes sting. Out of control. He'd lost control of himself, and he didn't know if he could pull himself together if they kept talking. His words were clipped, thick when he managed to say, "It took two months before he hit me the first time. He apologized as soon as he did it."

Bastian let out a slow exhale and clenched his hands around his biceps a few times. "And you figured he'd just gotten angry and screwed up, so you gave him a second chance."

There was repressed anger in Bastian's tone, and it struck a nerve. Riley had been a victim then, but he knew now that it hadn't been his fault. He'd be damned before he let Bastian say it was. "You think it's all my fault?"

"No!" Bastian's eyes widened. "I think it's what most people would do, give a second chance and try to forgive. I'm not pissed at you. I'm pissed that Jake had the nerve to hit you in the first place. Hitting's just... It's wrong. It completely breaks the trust. Only time it makes sense is during sex, if you're into that sort of kink, but that's controlled. It's not some fit of rage." Bastian clenched his jaw. "Did he hit you during sex, too?"

Riley's mouth went dry. Dozens of moments flickered in his mind's eye, those endless nights of Jake coaxing him into more and more extreme play that never really felt like play. "Yes," he said, voice tight.

"That's not all he did."

"No." Riley didn't want to go back there, back to those terrifying nights. In hindsight, he didn't know why he never just left, but he'd stayed. Like some fucked up moron, he'd stayed. What had been simple little things that had only made him uncomfortable in the beginning had swiftly become nightmarish pain, and there had been no safeword for him. "He liked to tie me up. Leave me there, naked, for hours. Sometimes all night. If I'd moved at all, made a sound or..." Riley shook his head, his vision blurring. "If I wasn't as he'd left me, it wasn't a great bout of sex for me."

Bastian squeezed his eyes shut and ran his hands through his hair. "And you didn't tell anyone besides Cheryl?"

Riley's eyes narrowed. "How do you know I told her?"

"She told me you cried over the phone to her about Jake when she threatened to kill me if I ever hurt you."

"She had no right to tell you that," Riley snapped. He'd confided in her, and then she'd gone and blabbed at Bastian. He swiped at his eyes before any of those bitter, useless tears could fall. He'd cried all he wanted about Jake and his choices back then. "Besides, who else would I tell? I kept thinking it would change, or maybe I was fucking up somehow. Jake was only my third boyfriend, and the second guy I'd had sex with. I wasn't well equipped to deal with his shit."

"No fuck up could be so bad you'd deserve that kind of treatment," Bastian insisted, taking another step closer. "How long? How long did this go on? What made you finally leave?"

Riley shifted on his feet, wanting run away from Bastian. Or was it run away from himself? Both. If he could *forget* all of this, live in the now, live in the happy warmth of Bastian's presence—vampire or not—the darkness Jake had put into his life wouldn't seem so terrible. "I put up with it for six... seven months." Such a short time for so much pain and lingering doubt to take root. "Cheryl helped me make the arrangements to transfer schools. Jake found out. He beat me. A lot. The neighbors heard me screaming and called the cops. They arrested him, but I wouldn't press charges." It was like all those other battered partner stories he'd heard on the news, and he'd become one of those pathetic statistics. It hadn't been his proudest moment. "Cheryl drove up that night, picked me up from the hospital, and we packed as much as would fit in her car, and I left. He hasn't tried to find me, but I didn't think he would."

"What made you finally leave, Riley?"

A sick feeling wormed its way through Riley. He looked away, ashamed of himself and the tears that finally made their way down his cheeks. "It wasn't the beatings or the humiliations or the... sexual stuff." Oh, those had been bad, but he'd been in love with Jake. A sick, sick part of him, he thought, still loved Jake even as the rest of his mind and heart hated the man. "I think I would have gone on taking it. It's so twisted, I know, but I depended on him. I *needed* him. I didn't have to work. Just go to school and make him happy. I took all his crap, everything he could do to me, and then he started fucking around behind my back. He found some twink who *liked* to play his crazy games. It wasn't the beatings, it was the *cheating*! How fucking sick is—"

He jerked with surprise when Bastian stepped close and pulled him into a hug. His first thought was to run, but this was Bastian, and Bastian was trying to understand. Riley even *wanted* Bastian to understand. Maybe, if Bastian could help exorcise Jake from his memory, he could help

Bastian come to terms with being a vampire. He hesitantly raised his arms, but the moment he started hugging back, he couldn't help but tighten his grip.

"I'm so sorry," Bastian muttered into his robe, his voice wavering in a way that just made Riley's eyes sting with more tears. "All those months you were hurting, and he didn't give a shit. I'm not like that. I'd never treat you like nothing. You have to believe me."

"I know," Riley whispered. "I know that. I made you wait. I kept everything from you until you proved yourself, and you did. I don't mean to flinch—" he managed to say before a sob filled his throat. He didn't want Bastian to pay endlessly for sins he'd not committed. He loved Bastian, and Bastian loved him, and it was *good*, so good, and Riley didn't want to lose that feeling.

"He twisted something inside, knotted it all up. It'll take time to untangle. I get that. It's why I didn't say anything, but I needed to know what he did." Bastian pulled back and ran his fingers over Riley's face, wiping away the tears gently. The touches made Riley's skin tingle. They were so tender, so starkly different from what he remembered of Jake. "You have to tell me if something sets you off, okay? We can work through it together. You're worth the effort. You always have been."

Damn his coloring, because Riley could feel another blush stealing across his cheeks. He took a deep breath, let it out slowly. A little bit of the heavy feeling in his gut had lifted, and Riley knew the next time Bastian asked him about Jake, it would be easier. "Now tell me," he said, meeting Bastian's gaze, "why you pretend you don't drink a quart of pig's blood in the morning? Why do you hide it from me?" The hiding had made it difficult for Riley to face.

He'd processed it, and better than he'd expected, honestly, but they couldn't keep up the charade. Bastian wasn't like normal guys, and the sooner they faced that fact together, the better.

Bastian opened his mouth to speak, but nothing came out. It took a few tries and a lot of eye shifting before he was able to admit, "Because it's embarrassing. I want to be like everyone else, be a normal, safe boyfriend. It's not like having a glass of tomato juice with breakfast."

"What is it like?" Riley pressed.

"It's like when you're starving and you find something that really hits the spot. You feel like you could eat and eat and never get tired of it because it just feels good all over. It's like that... plus a really good make-out session." Riley raised his eyebrows at that, and Bastian blushed. "'Cause it's always vaguely sexual even though it isn't about sex. I pretend I don't do it because I enjoy it. A lot... and I feel like I shouldn't."

Riley's brow furrowed, because that description was odd. Really odd. "Pig's blood is a turn on?"

"No." Bastian pulled back then, and he walked to the fridge. He snatched a bottle of the blood out and held it up. "Pig's. Cow's. Human's. It's just blood. It's the *blood* that's a turn on."

"Oh," Riley said, staring at the blood in Bastian's hand. His stomach turned a little as he thought about Bastian drinking the cold, semi-congealed blood, but he tried his damnedest to keep that from his face and voice. "Are you going to drink it now? Are you hungry?"

Bastian eyed the bottle, rolling it restlessly in his hands. "That's just the thing. Even when I binge, the hunger

I feel never goes away completely." He looked up at Riley, and there was fear in his eyes. "I'm *always* hungry."

Riley wet his lips, because he had a feeling he knew how to sate that hunger. The answer that niggled in the back of his mind both terrified and aroused him. "Were you hungry after you fed on that homeless guy?"

Shame flashed over Bastian's face, and then he turned away. Riley rested a hand on Bastian's shoulder, and tension made the muscles tremble ever so slightly under his grip. "I don't remember," Bastian ground out.

"Sebastian," Riley warned, not liking even the simplest of lies. There couldn't be any lies between them now, not if Riley was right. If he was right, then everything could changed for them, and he needed to trust Bastian. Bastian needed to trust him. Slowly, Bastian turned in his grip.

"The whole thing *was* fuzzy, but... no. I wasn't hungry. I was scared shitless, but I wasn't hungry anymore."

Riley nodded. "Because you were consuming what you are supposed to." He smiled ruefully. "It's like me trying to live off Coke and Twinkies. Yeah, it's food, but it never fills you up."

A muscle in Bastian's jaw twitched. "I'm not going to feed off humans."

"You could feed off one," Riley murmured, his heart racing in his chest as he made the suggestion.

"Riley," Bastian begged, his voice softer, weaker than before. The water bottle of blood crackled in Bastian's hands. "I shouldn't be hungry. I shouldn't want your blood. I drank a whole bottle before. I shouldn't..."

He thought to push. Riley was sure he could force Bastian to feed from him, here in the kitchen. The perfect little snack. He had the urge to laugh at that, but he swallowed it back. Riley nodded slowly and stepped back. "Clean up the kitchen," he whispered. Riley forced a smile onto his lips. "I need to get dressed. We're low on groceries. You can sift Zoe's litter box while I'm out, and then we can do laundry. Your shirts stink."

Riley ducked his head and left the kitchen. From the hallway, he could hear Bastian curse colorfully, but he shook his head. Bastian wasn't ready. Riley had been forced by Jake to do a lot he had never wanted to do, and he was still ashamed of most of it. He'd never willingly do that to Bastian. When, and if, Bastian was ready, he'd be there. For now, they could go on pretending.

Chapter Seven

"So the endorphins and enkephalins are the *endogenous* opioids that the body takes care of on its own, right?" Stephen asked, slouched over his textbook.

"Right," Riley nodded, flipping a few pages forward to the chapter on analgesics and anesthetics. "The endorphins are like natural morphine."

"That's what I need right now, morphine," Stephen groaned, his forehead making a loud thud as it collided with his textbook and the table underneath it.

Riley chuckled and patted his shoulder. "Just remember the difference between morphine and codeine. There's no way that isn't on the test."

"Morphine has the methyl group on the top."

"Sorry, Stephen," Riley apologized with a sympathetic grimace. "Other way around. Codeine has the methyl group; morphine has the simple hydroxide group. Just try to remember the codeine is complex." He put emphasis on the consonants, hoping the mnemonic would help Stephen. It always did the trick for him.

"Dammit," Stephen cursed, seeking solace in a large handful of cheese puffs and a swig of Mountain Dew. "Remind me again why we decided to take pharmacology when we're gonna be working on animals."

"Because we know we'll have to take the veterinary version in grad school, and this'll give us a head start. Plus, it brushes up our chemistry." Riley smiled at Stephen's continued cursing and paged through his notes. "All right. Time for us to work on chemical structure."

"Hell no," Stephen protested. "I'm not the artist here; that's your boy-toy's job. How long has he been in there, anyway? Doesn't he have to eat or take a piss like the rest of us?"

Riley stared at the wall that separated the living room from the spare bedroom that Bastian had taken over for his art projects. As far as he knew, Bastian was still in that room working on his paintings and sculptures. Stephen elbowed him when he didn't answer immediately, and he punched Stephen's shoulder in retaliation. "Of course he eats. I guess he just doesn't like interruptions when he gets in that artistic zone of his."

Riley had gone in there to bring Bastian a sandwich at lunch, but the look on Bastian's face had sent him back out in a hot minute. Bastian had done several art projects at their apartment before and never minded company. Maybe it was just the stress of finals, but the tension in the room seemed to solidify the air into a toxic slurry the moment he'd walked in.

He turned back to his textbook and grabbed a blank sheet of paper, handing one to Stephen. It was best if he just ignored it. Bastian was probably just stressed out. No big deal. God knew he wanted to rip his own hair out when it came to his Neurology and Ophthalmology class. When the finals were over, and the summer loomed ahead of them, things would return to normal. "Draw codeine," he told Stephen.

"Only if you draw chlorzoxazone," Stephen fired back with a smirk.

"That's not a hard one," Riley laughed. "You just like saying the damn name."

"So sue me. Gotta find *something* fun with all this..."

Stephen's voice trailed off oddly, and Riley looked up and followed Stephen's gaze to the corner. Bastian was standing at the opening of the hallway, his pottery apron spattered with clay. Reddish brown was smeared on Bastian's arms as well, though he'd obviously washed his hands. Riley's eyes locked with Bastian's, and the heat between them was immediate. Just a look from across the room and his body tightened pleasantly. His mouth went dry when Bastian stepped into the room.

It was like Stephen wasn't even there. Bastian was utterly focused on Riley, and the attention made Riley's pulse speed up. It only took Bastian a couple heartbeats to close the distance between them, and all he could do was gasp when his mouth was claimed in a deep, possessive kiss.

The kiss wasn't like any other kiss they'd shared. Bastian was proving something with this one, and Riley let him. He didn't pull back until his lungs burned for oxygen, and then panted, staring into Bastian's eyes. "I-I'm studying."

"Take a break."

Riley tore his eyes from Bastian and looked over his shoulder at Stephen. Stephen was already packing up his books and papers. He gave Riley a grin. "Hey, I know when I'm cramping someone's style. I'll catch up with you tomorrow night." Stephen looked at Bastian. "*No* interruptions then."

Bastian pulled Riley's face back toward his and, soon, Riley was drowning in another kiss. He barely heard the door shut behind Stephen. He wrapped his arms around

Bastian's neck and opened his mouth wide, allowing Bastian to deepen the kiss, taste all of him. In an instant, he was hard. They'd not had time for much sex, and even when they had managed a few moments together, it hadn't been quite right. Something had been off between them since that morning in the kitchen two weeks ago, and Riley just wanted to fix it.

This, he felt, was fixing it. Bastian's passion was suffocating, but Riley thought it was in the best of ways. He couldn't get enough of Bastian, and Bastian seemed more than happy to oblige as the kissing went on and on. Riley broke the kiss, gasping in air. "What–?"

"You were right," Bastian said, his words ragged and breathless. "Dammit, Riley, you were right all along." Bastian's hands tugged at his sweatshirt, pulling it up over his head. The moment his face was free of the fabric, he was caught in another kiss that made his head spin.

Riley struggled a little, pulling back from the grasping hands and demanding mouth. "Right?" Bastian's fingers found his nipples and pinched at them. Riley cried out, heat rushing through him as thinking became impossible for a silent, bright moment. He gathered his wits and pushed Bastian's hands away from him. Riley scooted to the other end of the couch and tried to catch his breath. "Right about *what*? What's going on?"

"I need blood. I'm a vampire. You're right that I'm denying what I am." Bastian reached for him, but Riley kept him at arm's length. Bastian took the cue and sat back, his fingers running almost compulsively through his hair. "I can't concentrate. I can't stop thinking about drinking from you. I can't be in the same room as you without hearing your pulse and feeling that hunger. It's driving me fucking crazy!"

Heat crept over Riley's cheeks. "I'm sorry," he murmured. This was his fault. He'd put the thought in Bastian's head. Bastian had managed to keep hold of something human for over a year now, and in one morning, Riley had ruined it. Tainted it with thoughts of his blood instead of the pig's. "What should we do?"

Bastian laughed, the sound hollow and unpleasant. "I don't know," he admitted. "I keep thinking if I drink more of the animal blood, this will go away."

Riley licked his lips and inched closer to Bastian on the couch. He didn't think that would actually solve the problem. The hunger would be there whenever Bastian woke up, when they made love, when they cuddled together to watch a movie. It was there, and they couldn't ignore it anymore. "It'll come back," he whispered. "You'll nuzzle my throat or kiss my wrist, and it'll come back."

"Every single time," Bastian groaned softly, eyeing Riley's slow advances. "I've gone through a few bottles of blood from my mini-fridge in the other room, but just you walking in..." Bastian shook his head. "I acted like an asshole, but it wasn't you. I've thought about it all day, and I've made up my mind."

Riley's heart leaped into his throat, and he stilled on the couch, just within Bastian's reach. Had things gotten so out of control for Bastian that he was going to leave? Panic sent a shiver down his spine, and he choked out, "About what?"

A muscle in Bastian's jaw twitched, and he watched Bastian's tongue dart out to wet his lips. "Is your offer still open? The offer you made in the kitchen the other morning?"

Bastian was going to do it. Bastian was going to drink from him. It had been something Riley's mind had turned to more and more the longer they were together. When Bastian would nip and suck at his throat as they fucked, the thought would appear vibrant and tempting in his mind. Would it hurt? Would it be amazing, like in books and movies? Would Bastian be able to control himself? Would it all go to hell in one moment, Bastian feeding until there was nothing left?

Riley took a deep breath and looked into Bastian's eyes. Need. He saw raw need in them, and fear. So much fear. It was fear he felt himself. Slowly, Riley nodded. "Yes," he breathed, and the word hung between them for a moment, as loud as thunder.

Bastian sighed, his entire body shifting with the controlled exhale. "You've gotta promise me something. Promise me you won't let me go too far. I don't have super strength or anything, so you'd better fucking hit me or something if I get out of control."

Riley cracked the smallest of smiles. Hit Bastian? The thought would have been laughable if Bastian weren't so serious about it. "I promise," he said, reaching over to brush his fingers over Bastian's cheek. The tension shuddered out of Bastian's shoulders at his touch. Bastian caught his hand before he could pull it away, and the reverent kiss Bastian placed over his pulse made his heart pound again. "How do you want to do this?"

"We don't have to do it any other way than we usually do," Bastian whispered against his wrist. "Come to bed with me."

"Now?"

Bastian nodded. "Now."

"What about your art stuff? Your final projects?" Riley didn't want Bastian to lose out on valuable, necessary work time just for a fucking and feeding, even if he really, really wanted to know what it was like.

"I nearly ruined my sculpture because my hand was shaking so bad. I need you now. The projects can wait," Bastian all but growled, the sound vibrating into Riley's wrist. Bastian stood and pulled him to his feet as well. "Do you care if I'm a little... dirty?" he asked, glancing at his clay-smeared skin.

Riley actually laughed. "You think you could wait long enough to shower if I said yes?"

Bastian grinned, showing his fully grown fangs. "Not really. We'll shower after... if we have the strength." He pulled Riley down the hall and into the bedroom. Bastian shooed Zoe off the bed, and then pulled off his paint and mud covered apron, rolling it up and tossing it into the bathroom. Even with the apron, Bastian's white tank top underneath was ruined, and it soon joined the apron. Riley watched, unable to look away. "Like what you see?" Bastian purred.

"Yes," Riley said. "You know I think you're gorgeous."

Bastian wrapped his arms around Riley's waist and kissed him again, this kiss much softer, slower. His toes curled with it, and Riley decided now was as good a time as any to experiment. He drew his tongue along a fang, moaning softly, and slid the tip of his tongue along the gum line. The reaction was instantaneous. Bastian cried out, his hands clutched him tightly, and the kiss became hungry and deep.

Riley's heart pounded as Bastian's hands slid up under his shirt and down into his jeans to squeeze his ass. They kissed until they were both reduced to panting pecks to one another's lips. Only then did Bastian pull away to yank off his own jeans.

"God, your pulse is fast," Bastian moaned, stepping free of his clothing. "I can hear it. I can smell your blood, feel it moving through you. I don't know how, but I do. It freaks me out, but it turns me on."

Hearing Bastian talk like that turned Riley on, too. Yes, he was afraid, but he wanted this so much. He was hard, and Bastian's cock was dark, heavy, ready to fuck him. It wouldn't be the only thing penetrating him today, and Riley groaned inwardly at the thought. He stripped, his hands unsteady as he bared his body to Bastian. "What does it smell like?" he asked, sitting on the edge of the bed, and then moving backward to the center of the mattress.

Bastian leaned against the edge of the bed on his arms, closed his eyes and inhaled deeply. There was something utterly feral in the movement that caused goosebumps break out over his skin, and he licked his lips when Bastian smirked. "Sweet but with those warm spices that everyone uses around the holidays. It's hot... musky... metallic. It's you in a way I don't know words for." Bastian's eyes opened, and he crawled onto the bed. "It draws me in, makes my cock ache."

"Bastian," Riley breathed. He was being seduced, but he didn't think Bastian was fully aware of it. Something had shifted in his lover. Shifted or broken. Whatever had happened inside Bastian's mind, it was reaching out to him now. His eyes followed Bastian's journey from the edge of the bed to between his legs. Within moments, he was trapped between the bed and Bastian, pinned by Bastian's lust and his own need. He tilted his head up, offered his lips, and they were instantly taken.

Riley's mind swam. Thinking was like walking through molasses. He kissed Bastian repeatedly, his hands wandering the trim, pale body above his. Riley was frantic by the time Bastian's lips made it to his throat, and he stared up at the bare, white ceiling. Just a few months ago, he'd ridden Bastian, knowing on one side of him lay the past, the other the future. He had that same, definitive feeling now. This would change things for both of them, for their relationship. It couldn't be taken back, and Riley knew, deep in his heart, he wouldn't want to.

Bastian sucked at his throat, moaned as he licked and nipped, and Riley yelped as cool, slick fingers pushed into his body. He hadn't even felt Bastian make a move for the lube.

"Even if the rest hurts," Bastian growled, "I'm gonna fuck you good."

All Riley could do was moan and spread his legs wider, and Bastian took full advantage, smearing the lube inside him with a few impatient thrusts and twists of his fingers. It was barely foreplay at all, but with Bastian's breath hot against his skin and those fangs scraping over his neck and shoulder, he didn't care.

"Riley," Bastian moaned at his throat, and then he surged forward with his body.

The clarity of the moment was startling. One moment Bastian's fingers were inside him, the next, he was filled by Bastian's cock. It was smooth, silken, and it was different. Riley gasped, his hands scratching down Bastian's shoulders. Bastian wasn't wearing a condom. Riley didn't understand why that mattered so much to him since Bastian was about to bite him, but it seemed like a much bigger deal in his mind than the biting and blood drinking.

"Bastian!" Riley cried out as Bastian withdrew and pushed back inside. His eyes rolled up in his head, and he wrapped his legs around Bastian. It was too late now. If there were consequences, he'd face them, but Bastian felt so good. So damn good, and he clung to Bastian, welcomed him in again and again.

His head fell back to the sheets, and he arched into the deep, possessive pace Bastian set. The movement stretched his neck out, and Bastian groaned unevenly against him. "I need... Can't wait..." Bastian's hands tightened at his shoulder and the nape of his neck.

The moment had come, and even with pleasure coursing through him, Riley couldn't help but tense. His eyes opened wide, an icy thrill of fear tingling down his spine. It was too late to stop, but he knew deep down he wanted this. Bastian sucked hard at his throat until his pulse pounded at the spot. Bastian's fangs pressed almost delicately against him, and he held his breath.

A moment later, Bastian struck, and all thought was impossible as pain slammed into him. If he cried out, he didn't hear himself. The pain radiated from his neck, ringing in his ears and making his body seize up. He squeezed his eyes shut tightly. He had figured it would hurt—someone biting into your throat should hurt—but not like this.

In the midst of it all, Bastian moaned and melted against him. Something caressed him, but it was a touch that didn't have a physical sensation to go with it. He didn't understand, but it was warm, inviting, and he gave into it without thinking. The pain disappeared almost as quickly as it had first hit him, and he gasped.

He grew still beneath Bastian, and it was a stillness that he was unable to fight. Unwilling to fight. Pleasure slowly seeped into his mind, hot and undeniable, and he moaned, his arms and legs twitching around Bastian. All he wanted to do in that moment was feed Bastian, give to him everything he was, and wallow in the pleasure that spilled over his senses.

Bastian's movements had softened, and Riley's eyes fluttered as they rocked gently into one another. That inner warmth wavered and slowly dissipated when Bastian pulled back from his throat, and he stared up at the bloodstained lips, the dazed hazel eyes, the healthy flush that had spread over Bastian's face.

Awareness seeped into Bastian's eyes, and concern overshadowed the pleasure on his face. "Riley," he panted, licking his lips. "Are you...?"

Riley reached for him, tried to pull him back down. He wanted to feed Bastian. There was no way Bastian could be full, sated, and that touch inside whispered for him to press the dangerous mouth back to his throat. "Bastian–"

Bastian resisted and shook his head. "Riley, no. I've... I've had enough." He rolled his hips forward, and Riley was drawn back to the physical moment.

The inner sense released his mind just a little, enough for him to groan and arch up. "Please," he panted. It was a fire inside him. Riley was restless, his ache in his balls now apparent as his mind cleared little by little. They weren't done. Somewhere inside him, a key had been turned, but the door had not opened. He didn't know how to open it, to quiet the uneasiness that seeped through his senses, and Riley decided the best way to shut it up was for Bastian to fuck him as promised. "God, please!"

Bastian moaned deep in his chest and thrust with a bit more power. Riley tightened his legs around Bastian's waist, pulling him deeper and willing away Bastian's uncertainty. It must have done the trick, because a smile slowly crept onto Bastian's face. The pace resumed, deep and claiming, and Riley's cry was muffled as Bastian pressed their lips together.

The kiss was hesitant. Bastian was uncertain. Would he want to taste his own blood on Bastian's tongue? As Bastian took him, that was the unspoken question between them, and Riley sought to answer as best he could. He parted his lips and thrust his tongue between Bastian's, holding tightly as the coppery flavor filled his own mouth. He'd have to learn to enjoy it, but it was Bastian. He... loved... Bastian, right? That meant all of him, even the dark parts.

Bastian kissed him back, practically purring into his mouth. There was nothing dark about the way Bastian curled his tongue around Riley's. It was tender, sensual, and when Bastian's hand closed around his cock and stroked him, he could tell that even the dark parts didn't change the way Bastian felt about him. He bucked into Bastian's grip, giving himself over to the pleasure of being pressed so close without any barrier between them.

Riley gasped into another kiss. Bastian's hand and cock worked in tandem to drive him crazy. He squeezed his eyes shut until he saw stars. His whole body was tight as a bowstring, trembling with the tension, and then the bowstring snapped. Riley shouted as he bucked, his hands clawing at Bastian's neck. Flames licked at him, hot and intoxicating, and he let himself drown in it, dimly aware of Bastian pushing into him faster, harder, both of them careless with passion.

Bastian's shout echoed in his ears, and his own breath hitched when wetness spread inside him. His muscles clenched as Bastian's thrusts slowed. It was smooth, hot and smooth, just like he remembered. But this time, it wasn't one of Jake's punishments. It wasn't a perverted intrusion. It was everything it should have been: intense, pleasant, and undeniably intimate.

Bastian's hold on his cock slipped, and the hand snaked under him, wrapping around his waist. The solid weight of Bastian's body against his, pressing him into the bed, was exquisite. Bastian felt warm, far warmer than he could ever remember him being. Riley forced himself from the haze of the afterglow, lifting his head to look down at Bastian. His neck protested, but he managed a glimpse of Bastian before resting his head again. It hadn't just been his imagination. Bastian was flushed, healthy, and more alive than ever.

"Riley," Bastian murmured, his voice thick as he shifted above Riley, brushing Riley's hair back from his face. "God, Riley. Are you all right? I didn't... You're okay?"

Riley blinked a couple of times, and then reached up to card his fingers through Bastian's hair. His limbs were heavy. It was almost as if he were drunk. "I'm all right," he said, a goofy grin spreading over face. "I'm fucking fantastic."

Bastian nuzzled his throat. "Fucking fantastic?" he said, and Riley heard such relief in his lover's words.

"Yeah," Riley slurred. "Fucking *fantastic*."

"Me, too," Bastian laughed, peppering kisses over his jaw, neck, and shoulder. "I feel overheated and alive and... God, I love you!" Bastian licked over one of his nipples, and he squirmed lethargically. One thing Bastian obviously didn't feel was tired, but Riley couldn't help but smile.

"I love you, too, but if you're expecting another round or two, the answer's no."

Bastian hovered over him, and the look of adoration in those eyes made Riley's heart skip a beat. "Think you can handle a quick shower? I've kinda made a mess of you."

Riley groaned. He knew he was a mess, and his throat was starting to seriously hurt, but he just wanted to curl up and go to sleep. It was as if he'd run a marathon or been up for two days straight. Exhaustion tugged at him. "I don't know. I just want to go to sleep. I'm so very tired now." He felt Bastian's weight move off him, but even his eyelids felt too heavy to lift. Riley wanted to roll over, sleep the day away.

"Riley, wait just a few more minutes," Bastian called. Called? How far away was Bastian?

Riley heard water run, a door open. He didn't want a shower. Didn't he say that? He tried to force his throat to work, but it wouldn't. His body was in full rebellion, determined to slip into dreams now that everything he had to give had been taken.

"Riley? Riley, come on now."

Riley sighed. "I just wanna sleep, Bastian. Let me sleep."

"Just stay awake a little bit longer. I want to get you cleaned up. You're a mess, and I can't let you..."

He didn't hear anything else. Sleep claimed him, dragging his drained mind and body under dark waters. It wasn't like any other sleep, deep and unmoving with hidden things lurking in the shadows. Riley walked the line between dreams and nightmares, unaware of Bastian's tending of his body as the sun sank below the horizon.

Riley squinted up at the sky, which was overcast and dreary. Some might think it a crappy day, but Riley rather liked it. It meant he could have lunch, outside, with his boyfriend. He smiled at Bastian and took another bite of his sandwich. "You didn't have to come out," he murmured.

Bastian nudged him, not quite as bundled up as he usually was. "I wanted to. We almost never have the chance to be outside in the daylight together." Bastian was quiet for a moment as a couple with an umbrella rushed past their bench in the park. When they were alone again, he turned to Riley. "I also want to talk about what's been going on with you."

The day could have been perfect, Riley supposed, if it hadn't started with him waking up in a cold sweat and a scream on his lips. The nightmares were intense, so real to him, and they'd begun the second time he'd fed Bastian. Each time he fed him, the nightmares became worse. Now, every time he went to sleep, he was plagued by darkness, blood, and creatures that bore no resemblance to anything in life. Part beast, part demon, part something he couldn't identify, but they had sharp teeth, inhuman eyes, and no care for the pain as they tore at his flesh in the shadowed haze of his dreams.

"It's nothing," he muttered. "Just some bad dreams. It happens." Riley tossed his half-eaten sandwich back into his lunch sack, his appetite soured.

"But it's happened more than once," Bastian pointed out. "When I woke up before you a few days ago, you were restless. Both nights were right after I'd..." Bastian peered around them quickly, lowering his voice. "After I'd fed from you. Was this going on before that, or is it connected somehow to what we've been doing?"

Riley clenched his jaw, which caused the muscles in his neck to tighten and the healing bite on his throat to ache. It reminded him of the mind-blowing fucking and feeding they'd done before he'd passed out last night. He didn't want Bastian to know the nightmares had plagued him through finals and into summer break. Something inside him warned if Bastian knew, the feedings would stop, and he couldn't let that happen. "It's just some nightmares. Don't make this into a bigger deal than it is."

Bastian's eyes narrowed, and the discerning glint in them made Riley shift unconsciously. Riley knew that look. It was the look Bastian got when there was a strong chance Riley wasn't telling the whole truth. He was a shitty liar, but Bastian had a way of knowing when he was being even a little dishonest. It was annoying as hell. He sighed. "Just because they started around the same time doesn't mean they're linked, Bastian."

"But they could be," Bastian protested. "This isn't cool. Your sleeping soundly is way more important than me feeding. I've got plenty of blood in the fridge, so I can make do with less from you. Your whole college and grad school career could go down the tubes."

"It won't go down the tubes. I'll manage," Riley snapped. He'd told Bastian not to overreact. Obviously, he wasn't getting the message across. Bastian's jaw twitched, his eyes darting around the lawn. At least his tone made Bastian hesitate.

"I'm just worried. Remember a month or so ago, when you told me about one of the animals in the clinic having a bunch of problems all because it wasn't sleeping well?" Riley opened his mouth to protest, but Bastian cut him off, holding up his hand between them. "No. Don't tell me this is different. It's a different situation, sure, but it's sorta the same thing. Don't get me wrong, I *love* drinking from you." Bastian's eyes darted down to his neck, and it made Riley's pulse speed up. "I love it, but maybe we should cut back a little and see if that helps your sleep."

"No!" Panic swelled in Riley, threatening to strangle him. "I don't *want* to cut back. I don't need to either. I can pick up some melatonin or something to help with the sleep issues. There isn't any good reason to stop."

He didn't want to stop. He couldn't. Riley needed to feed Bastian. Jealousy and fear swirled inside him at the idea of his blood being replaced by some dead pig's. He was better. Bastian was always so warm and alive after he fed him, and he liked Bastian alive. He liked Bastian happy, and when Bastian was sated and flushed and warm, Riley knew it was because of him. No one else. Just him. And that thing inside him, that instinct that had risen inside him after the first feeding, demanded he feed Bastian.

Bastian's touch at his shoulders made him jump, and he met Bastian's concerned eyes as those hands squeezed rhythmically at his shoulders. "I'm not saying we stop completely. I don't think I could quit even if I wanted to." A smile twitched at Bastian's lips. "You're part of me now in a really deep, personal, hard to describe sort of way. I'm not about to lose that. I'm just trying to look out for you."

The tension that had just started to ease out of Riley's shoulders came back instantly, twice as bad as before. "I can look out for myself."

"You can, but you're not," Bastian muttered, and Riley was glad Bastian's hands fell away from his shoulders. It saved him the trouble of pushing Bastian away.

Riley stood up and grabbed his coat. "I eat. I sleep. I work. I study. I manage to have sex with you half a dozen times a week, too, alongside feeding you. I think, Sebastian, I'm doing a fine job of looking out for myself."

Bastian winced, and Riley looked away before any sort of hurt could appear on Bastian's face. The last thing he needed right now was to feel guilty for something he'd said. He had no reason for guilt. He had to feed Bastian, and that was exactly what he planned on doing. There was a blessed moment of silence, and as he snatched up his lunch sack, he half thought Bastian would just let him walk away. He turned to leave, but Bastian's hand on his wrist stopped him. "What?" he snapped, glaring down at Bastian.

"You'd let me drain you dry without ever thinking we need to ease up, wouldn't you?"

Riley felt the flush creep up his throat and over his cheeks. He pulled his hand away from Bastian. "Of course not," he said thickly. But he wasn't sure. It wasn't a lie, but it wasn't the truth either, and it frightened Riley. "I have to go. Lunch break is over. I'll see you at home."

Bastian closed his eyes for a moment, and then sighed, his shoulders slumping. "Yeah. I'll see you there. Dinner'll be waiting. My turn to cook tonight."

Riley nodded and turned away. He hated that defeated look on Bastian's face, even if it meant he'd won and the discussion was over. A low rumble of thunder sounded above him, and he looked up at the cloudy skies. If he wanted to ride his bike home tonight, he'd have to do it in the rain. He shrugged on his coat and started off down the sidewalk, not even looking back. Riley knew what he'd see, and if he didn't walk away now, he'd say fuck it to his job, go home with Bastian, and make up for this fight.

As angry as he was, Riley knew there was truth to Bastian's words. Maybe they had a problem. Maybe this wasn't as simple as sex and fangs. Maybe there was something they simply didn't know because Bastian had never thought to ask the questions. The first spatters of rain fell on his face as he reached the clinic, and he yanked open the door before the sky opened up on him. He'd ask Bastian tonight... after he apologized for being a complete and utter asshole.

Bastian

Chapter Eight

The metallic tap of Bastian's knife against the wooden table was getting really old, and Bastian set it aside so he'd stop fiddling with it like a stir-crazy idiot. He looked up at the clock again before he could stop himself, and even though the minute hand had only moved over five tiny marks since he'd last checked, he still groaned. He'd put dinner back in the oven exactly forty-seven minutes ago to stay warm.

Riley was usually so uptight about being on time. Punctuality was practically his middle name. Bastian knew they'd argued, but that wasn't enough of a reason for Riley to be over an hour late getting home, was it? Bastian ran his hands through his hair and rubbed at the back of his neck.

A soft jingle caught his attention over the light pattering of the rain outside, and he leaned back in his seat to look around the corner into the living room. Zoe was pacing back and forth in front of the tiled entryway. She stopped after a few seconds, sitting and looking up at the doorknob. God, even the cat was waiting for Riley to come back.

"Zoe," he called, making a kissing noise with his lips. Her ears twitched his direction, but she still stared up at the door. "He's just a little late, Zoe. Come here." He beckoned her with a scratching motion of his hand near the floor, and she trotted over with a loud meow. He picked her up and cuddled her on his lap. "It's all right. He probably just stopped at the store or something on his way home. Maybe they had him stay late, cover someone else's ass for not showing up."

Zoe purred and nuzzled him, but it didn't stop his stomach from tying itself in knots. The more excuses he came up with, the more improbable all of them sounded. Riley had a cell phone, dammit. He could have called if he was going to be late. That left him with two options, and both bothered him. On the one hand, Riley could be keeping him waiting on purpose to get back at him for bringing up the whole nightmare problem. Riley wasn't a vindictive man, though. They'd had their spats in the past, but it usually ended with amazing make-up sex, not one of them going missing in action.

On the other hand, something else could have happened, could have kept Riley from getting home. He shuddered and pushed the thought away. He hugged Zoe until she struggled in his arms and jumped down to sit by the front door again.

There were a million totally legitimate reasons Riley could be late. He smiled and shook his head. "He's fine," he told himself. "He'll be home any minute, and then you'll feel like even *more* of a dumbass."

He jumped out of his seat with a loud yelp when the phone rang. His heart hammered in his throat, and he laughed off the tension as he reached for the phone. See? There was the phone call now. He'd just been jumping the gun. He leaned against the wall as he pressed the button on the phone and held it to his ear. "Riley?"

"No."

Cheryl. It was Cheryl, and she sounded like she had a cold. "Cheryl, I'm sorry, but Riley isn't home right now. I'll let him know you called."

"Bastian," she said, and then paused. "You need to come to UT Medical Center."

Bastian's heart dropped in his chest. Was the floor still beneath him? His head spun, those words echoing in his mind. "Why?"

Cheryl sniffled and exhaled slowly. "There was an accident. James is already here. You've met James, right? Riley's brother? He thought I should call you. Tell you. Riley is in surgery."

Bastian froze in place, and for a terrifying moment, his blood ran cold through him. "Oh, God," he whispered into the phone. A tremor started in his hands and worked its way up to his torso. His throat tightened, and he pushed off the wall to pace the length of the kitchen. "Surgery? What kind of surgery? Is he okay? It's just a broken bone or something, right?" Cheryl didn't answer immediately, and Bastian's heart went into overdrive, throbbing in his ears. "Right?"

"There are broken bones, and they're setting those." Cheryl sighed. "He wasn't responsive when they brought him in. There's... swelling. In his brain. You need to come down here."

All the air left his lungs in a rush, and he dashed into the entryway, nearly tripping over Zoe as he scrambled to pull on his jacket. He gasped for breath and squeezed his eyes shut. He had to focus, had to pull himself together and make sense of his scattered thoughts. He forced himself to breathe deeply, and then brought the phone back to his ear.

"I'm on my way," he choked out. God, was his voice really that high? He shook his head to clear it and grabbed his keys from the peg by the door. He paused with his hand near the doorknob. A curse left him as he ran back to the kitchen to shut the oven off and take the tea kettle off the heat. The last thing he needed was for the whole place to go up in flames.

Instead of fishing through his backpack for his wallet, he just threw the whole thing onto his shoulders. A few seconds later, he was out the door, not even caring that he still had the phone in his hand. When he brought it back up to his ear, all he heard was the dial tone. Cheryl had hung up. He stuffed the phone in his jacket pocket.

"I'm on my way, Riley," he panted as he jogged through the rain to the closest bus stop. "Just hold on.

Bastian threw back the hood of his jacket, sending a spray of raindrops behind him as he rushed into the Emergency Room area and up to the receptionist. "Riley Lynch, ICU?" he asked, frantic. She pointed him down a hallway, and he walked as quickly as he could, his sneakers squeaking against the tiles with every step.

The bus ride had been torturous. Whenever they'd reached another stop along the route, he'd debated if it would be faster to get off and just run the rest of the way. He'd managed to stay put, though, and the half hour ride had felt like an eternity. He needed to see Riley, needed to hold his hand and tell him it was going to be all right, even if it wasn't true.

When he turned the corner into the waiting room, he immediately spotted Cheryl and crossed to her. He called out to her, and she turned to face him. Her face was splotchy, her eyes red from tears, and just seeing her in such a state made his own eyes sting. "Any news?"

"He's resting. I can't go in," Cheryl said, wiping her cheeks. "James... says he hasn't woken up. The doctor isn't sure how long he'll be out."

Bastian's face contorted, and he pulled Cheryl into a hug as guilt tightened his chest painfully. "He has to wake up," he whispered against her shoulder. "I have to tell him I'm sorry, that I love him."

"You're sorry?" Cheryl pulled back, frowning at him. "You mean, you're sorry you upset him? That you made him feel like he couldn't juggle you and his life? Or that you're sorry you're just as controlling an asshole as Jake, trying to manipulate Riley into doing what you want when you want?"

Bastian gawked at her, and his chest ached as if she'd stabbed him. "What are you talking about? I didn't manipulate him into anything." His whole body felt cold except for a spark of anger that took hold in his gut. He clenched his hands into tight fists. "I didn't force him into anything!"

But if he hadn't done anything wrong, then why did doubt rise up in him? Why did he start thinking of their argument, of all the little things they'd argued about or the misunderstandings that had come and gone? They'd made mistakes, sure, but was he really as bad as Jake? He shook his head, trying to hold onto his anger. It was so much easier to be pissed off than to think that everything was his fault.

"He said you had lunch today, that you were thinking of taking something from him." Cheryl glared.

"Riley said it was *important*. That you didn't want him to have it as often or something. He was very vague, but I know the kind. I know how giving and bendable Riley is." She poked Bastian in the chest. "I wouldn't have even called you if James hadn't insisted!"

"I'm his boyfriend!" Bastian hissed at her, and for a moment, he seriously considered screaming the truth of the whole situation at her, telling her everything. The moment passed, but the thought had been there. He couldn't tell her. He'd been able to trust Riley with his secrets, but he couldn't trust anyone else, especially Cheryl when she was this pissed off. She'd just think he was a monster and have him locked up or sent to the psycho ward. The thought that she wouldn't have even called him made him seethe. "Maybe what he wanted was dangerous for him. Maybe I thought he might hurt himself or that it was too much of a good thing. One argument between us, and you think I'm like Jake, but I'm not! The only reason I brought it up to him at all was because I was worried about *him*."

Bastian ran his hands through his hair, pausing to pull at it as he sank into one of the seats lining the wall. "You think it doesn't hurt to know the last things we said to one another were on the tail end of an argument? I know you love him and worry about him, but is it so hard to believe that I do, too?"

Cheryl glared at him, but her eyes were filled with tears. "Riley called just before he left."

Bastian wet his lips. "What did he say?"

"That you have fought. That you were trying to take something from him, but he knew something was off. He wouldn't tell me what, but he promised to call Monday." Cheryl looked away, swiping at a tear. "Riley said he had to get home and fix things. He was rushing home in the rain, in the dark, because he was so upset you were upset. I love him, Bastian. He's like a brother to me, but you... I barely know. He wanted to get home to you, and he was hit by a fucking car."

The guilt inside Bastian rose up to choke him, and he leaned forward onto his elbows. His backpack was in the way, restricting the movement of his arms, and he struggled to get it off his arms, the wet fabric of his jacket clinging to it. The effort it took just to get the bag off and to the floor made all the other emotions worse, and some small control inside of him snapped. His shoulders shook as he squeezed his eyes shut. "It's my fault, then, isn't it?" he choked out. "All I'd wanted was for us to work it out together. I swear, Cheryl. I didn't want this to happen."

"It's not your fault," Cheryl murmured. Her arms were crossed over her ample chest, her eyes focused on the doors that led back into the ICU. "You weren't driving that car. You didn't hit Riley."

Bastian nodded mutely and rocked a couple times in his seat before he stood up again. He couldn't just sit there. He couldn't just wait and cry and hope. "I have to see him," he muttered, wiping at his eyes. "I have to do something. Anything." But there wasn't much he could do. Cheryl was practically Riley's sister, but they hadn't let her back to see Riley. He probably didn't have much of a chance. Cheryl licked her lips, her eyes darting up to him. "What?" he asked. "Have you been back to see him?"

"No," she said. "I'm not family. But, you're his partner." Cheryl stood, picked up the hospital phone in the waiting room, and dialed a number. After a moment, she spoke softly to whoever picked up the phone. "He's here." A silent moment. "He wants to see him." She made an agreeable sound and hung up. Cheryl sat down in her seat again. "James will be out in a minute to get you."

Bastian's breath shuddered out of him, and he sat next to Cheryl, pulling her into a hug. "Thank you. I know we're not close, but you're still my friend. You're really important to Riley, too." A bit of the tension in Cheryl's shoulders eased, and he held her tighter. "You should be able to go up there, too. You're not some random friend; you're like family."

"I'll go in when Maggie and Scott get here." Cheryl held up her cellphone. "They're on the road now."

The doors opened, and a man Bastian hadn't had the opportunity to meet yet waited in the doorway. "Sebastian?"

Bastian stood up, nervous. "Yeah. You're James?"

James held out his hand. "I'm sorry we had to meet like this. I'd have preferred Thanksgiving dinner, not an ICU ward."

Bastian managed a weak smile and shook James' hand before following him through the doors. "Me, too. Riley tried to get me to come with him last November. I wish I had." His own family had demanded a visit, though, and he had been so nervous about meeting Riley's relatives. It all seemed so petty now.

James led him back through the ward until they reached the right room, and Bastian paused at the door. He closed his eyes and took a couple deep breaths. He knew it would be bad, but he still had to prepare himself before he opened his eyes and walked in. It took a few seconds for the whole scene to sink in, for the tubes and wires and slings to make sense, and Bastian's vision wavered with tears as he rounded the hospital bed. He wiped them away as he stood next to the bed.

Riley's right arm and leg were wrapped in braces and elevated. Bastian reached over to take Riley's other hand, careful not to disturb the monitor on Riley's finger or the IV that was attached to his wrist. "Oh, God, Riley," he whispered, his eyes scanning over Riley's bruised face and the bandages pressed against his forehead and shoulder. Just seeing Riley's deathly pale skin and holding his cool hand made Bastian's chest ache, but it was hearing Riley's pulse that made him bite back a soft sound of grief. He'd gotten so used to Riley's heartbeat, a strong, steady thrum in his ears when they were together. Now, it was weak, so much fainter than before, barely stable. He didn't need the beeping monitors to tell him Riley was in bad shape. He could feel it in the way his blood moved, struggling to heal all those injuries at the same time.

He forced himself to swallow and breathe, sniffling as he took a seat in the chair that James scooted forward for him. "I'm here, Riley," he murmured, trying to control his voice.

"They relieved the pressure on his brain as much as they could," James murmured. "His spleen had been lacerated, and Dr. Rhodes said we're lucky they got him here so quickly. They had to remove it, but... he's lost a lot of blood, Sebastian. Dr. Rhodes said he'd talk to everyone in the morning, but these first twenty-four hours would tell us if the damage done was just too much." James' voice wavered for a moment, and then he cleared his throat. "They've done what they can for now. Mom and Dad should be here in the morning."

Bastian nodded without looking up at James. He was sure he'd just see a mirror image of his own expression, drawn tight with worry and grief. "Can I stay overnight?" he asked softly with a sniffle. "Would it bother you?"

"No," James murmured, and a warm hand squeezed Bastian's shoulder. "You can stay." James leaned over Riley to gently brush back a few strands of red hair from bruised skin. Bastian glanced over and caught a small, watery smile on James' face. "Cameron and I heard nothing but good things about you at Christmas. Maybe having you here with him will help."

Bastian returned the small smile. He gently squeezed Riley's hand, his eyes scanning Riley's face for any hint of change or improvement. "I hope so," he whispered.

Bastian jolted awake to the sound of the blood pressure monitor changing pitch. He groaned into the sheets of Riley's bed. He'd fallen asleep on his watch again.

Shit, he'd fallen asleep!

Straightening in his seat caused a sharp pain to shoot down his back into his legs, but he barely noticed as his heart raced. His eyes quickly took in Riley's face and body, and when he didn't see anything different, he looked at the machines. He'd gotten quite good at reading them the last three weeks. Riley had changed rooms a couple times, but at least the equipment stayed the same. Heart rate was good, blood pressure the same as usual, and vitals stable.

He breathed a sigh of relief and slumped back in his seat again. No matter how many times the machines woke him up, it always scared the shit out of him. "God, do you have to keep doing that?" he asked Riley's unconscious form with a small smile. "You're gonna send me into the bed right next to you with some sort of heart attack. Bet the doctors would have a field day then, huh?"

The amusement faded as he stared at Riley's face. The bruises had healed up, the abrasions were mostly gone, the broken bones were mending, but the expression hadn't changed one bit. He'd watched Riley's mom and dad hug Riley and whisper how much they loved him. He'd listened from right outside as Cameron had an entire conversation with Riley, but even a visit from Riley's little twin nephews hadn't changed the look on his face.

Bastian was grateful for all of them in a way he hadn't expected. He was never pushed aside, never made to feel unimportant by anyone in Riley's family. Maggie, Riley's mother, had been very focused on ensuring he ate, slept, and went outside periodically. It was a sweet, motherly gesture that Bastian barely remembered from his own mom. They'd accepted him, talked with him, let him hug them if they broke down and supported him whenever he had his own moments of grief. They'd even let him sit in on the meetings with Dr. Rhodes.

Riley had officially slipped into a coma. He wasn't brain dead—they had plenty of test results to prove that much—but he just wouldn't wake up. The swelling and bruising in his brain had passed, but Riley remained stoically unconscious. Bastian had tried everything he could think of, short of bringing in Zoe, which was against hospital rules. Nothing had fazed Riley, and they had all finally been gathered together for a serious talk with Dr. Rhodes.

There had been a lot of medical jargon that Bastian didn't understand, but what he'd heard clearly was that the longer Riley stayed in the coma, the less of a chance he had of coming out of it. There was also the worry that there could be permanent brain damage left over even if he came to again, and that would only get worse as time went on.

The thought brought tears to his eyes as he combed his fingers through Riley's hair. "I thought you'd wake up within a couple days," he mumbled to Riley. "You keep proving me wrong, like you're trying to get some point across." He just wished he knew what that point was. That it was Riley's time and he just needed to let go? He shook his head furiously at the thought. He wasn't going to lose Riley. He couldn't. They hadn't had enough time together!

But as the weeks wore on, his doubts were growing. He'd pulled out of his summer school class in order to take longer shifts at his job. If he'd had a choice, he'd have spent more time in the hospital, but he had to pay the bills and feed Zoe, not to mention fill his own need for blood. Animal, of course—he had no intention of feeding from anyone else.

Just the thought of blood made his thirst gnaw at his insides, and his mind kept cycling back to the argument he'd had with Riley before everything went to hell. He didn't bother blaming himself anymore, but that had been the first time he'd ever wondered if they needed help from someone else. From another vampire.

He'd forgotten about the thought for the first few weeks, expecting Riley to wake up any day, but now...

Bastian grimaced as he leaned forward to kiss Riley's unresponsive lips. "I'd do anything to save you," he whispered, and the truth behind the words made him shiver a little as he sat on the edge of the bed and held Riley's hand.

He'd tried everything in the last few weeks, but none of it had done any good, and when his mind played over their argument again, a single thought burned in his mind. He had been trying to do everything he could as a human, but was that the same thing as what he could do as a vampire? The two of them had never found any special powers connected to the changes in him, other than his enhanced senses. Then again, he had always tried too hard to be normal at the same time.

Was he missing something? Was there something he was overlooking because he'd never really explored being a vampire? He couldn't answer those questions, and it was starting to nag at him. He didn't think there was any magical hocus pocus that went along with his pointy teeth, but what if there was?

There was only one way to find out, and he didn't like it. It meant finding another vampire and asking, but the only vampire he knew of was the asshole who had changed him. That was one encounter he didn't want to relive, but as he looked at Riley again, he felt the chill of panic making his heart pound. They were running out of options.

He glanced over at his sketch book and pencils, which he always brought with him for his shifts of watching over Riley. He'd just said he would do anything to save Riley. It was time to live up to that promise. He picked up his pencils, opened to a blank page and started drawing.

Chapter Nine

The evening was warm and muggy, the humidity lingering from a full day that had promised rain but never delivered. It was rather miserable, but Bastian reminded himself that it could have been much worse. After all, he could be hanging flyers in the middle of the afternoon, sweating his ass off with every inch of him covered to protect him from the sun. Compared to that, the night was just peachy.

Industrial stapler in hand, Bastian stepped close to one of the poles on campus that people informally used for party invites. Pulling a flyer out of his backpack, he stapled it to the post and stepped back. It was right where it needed to be in the light, but the face that stared back at him on the page made him shiver and a pit of unease form low in his gut.

Bastian supposed that was a good reaction; it meant his drawing was lifelike enough to pull up his emotions. He could remember every detail of that face. He might have been a little tipsy when they'd started fooling around, but there's nothing like being turned into a vampire to make you pay attention to your attacker's face. He'd taken a few days to get the drawing just right, and now it was posted up all over campus.

It was a long shot, since the party crowd usually wasn't the same crowd that stuck around for summer school, and it had been a year since the party, but it was better than doing nothing. He had hit the fraternity houses first. Most of the fraternity houses didn't even have huge parties, but he'd wanted to retrace his steps, so it had felt like the logical place to start, even with most of the students gone for the summer.

There was always the chance that the man who had turned him into a vampire was long gone, too. He obviously hadn't been too attached to Bastian, so there was no reason to suspect that he was still in Knoxville. Bastian couldn't help but smile grimly as he walked to the next well-lit post to hang another flyer. On the other hand, he couldn't think of a reason for the guy to leave, either. Maybe this was his territory. Bastian was counting on it.

His phone vibrated in his pocket just as he was about to staple up the next flyer, and he immediately dug it out of his pocket and looked at the number. 'Private', was all his phone blinked up at him. That definitely wasn't the hospital or any of his friends. Hell, Cheryl even had her own special ringtone on his phone these days. It set off little flags in his mind, but he pushed the button to answer anyway.

"Hello?"

"Sebastian Rossi?"

Bastian frowned as he juggled the stapler, flyers, and phone. The soft, male voice on the other end of the line wasn't one he was familiar with. "Yeah?"

"I represent a party who has recently seen your slew of unnecessary advertisements for a member of their community. I was instructed to respond to your call for information."

His heart pounded in his chest. A lead! "What information can you give me?"

"I am sorry, none. I can give you an address, and then you must decide if you will meet with my employer or not. But, be advised, by morning, your flyers will have been removed. They will be removed each night you put them up."

Bastian glared at the face staring back him from his flyer. "I need to find this asshole."

"I understand that, Mr. Rossi, but there are rules you are breaking. We understand your situation, and that is why I was told to respond to your cry for help. 231 Sixth Avenue North, Mr. Rossi, in Nashville. Come tomorrow night. When you go to the front desk, ask for the Presidential Suite."

"Nashville?" Bastian shook his head. "I can't go to Nashville. My lover is in the hospit-"

"Yes, we are aware of Mr. Lynch's current predicament." That voice was so artificially understanding that it grated on Bastian's nerves. "We will have a driver waiting for you at your residence tomorrow at sunset. We will be sure to return you in the same condition you arrive in."

Bastian swallowed thickly and shifted his phone over to the other ear. He clenched his jaw, biting back questions he was pretty sure wouldn't be answered by this nameless guy over the phone. Just how much did these people know? He'd only started putting up the posters a few hours ago. How could someone find out about him and Riley so quickly when Riley was in the hospital? He shook his head. He'd drive himself crazy with all those questions right now.

"How the hell can I trust anything you say? This driver could take me to the middle of nowhere just so you, or whoever you work for, can shoot me dead." Bastian didn't know if that could really kill him, if his being a vampire meant he could only be killed in certain ways, but he didn't exactly want to find out the hard way.

The man's voice took on an amused tone. "Mr. Rossi, do you want your answers or not?"

Bastian ground his teeth together. He couldn't throw away the opportunity. Riley's life might depend on him taking the chance. "Yeah, I want my answers, but if I'm going to take a risk, you've gotta do the same. I need some sort of..." He struggled to find the phrase. "A pledge of good faith."

"You are hardly in a position to bargain."

"Humor me," Bastian insisted.

"Tomorrow at sunset, Mr. Rossi," the man said, and then the line went dead.

Bastian stared at the screen as it blinked a couple times and returned to his normal wallpaper. "Mother fucker!" he growled at it.

He shoved his flyers back into his backpack with his phone and seethed. It wasn't just because he'd been hung up on, but because he knew he didn't have much choice in the matter if he wanted to know what he set out to learn. He glared at the flyer on the pole in front of him and pounded staples into the man's eyes. It didn't do him any good, but it made him feel better as he stalked back toward the bus stop on the edge of the campus.

The taxi cab lurched over a bump in the street, and Bastian swore under his breath. The three hour drive from Knoxville to Nashville had been harrowing, mainly due to his own nerves. As they rounded another street, Bastian was certain a heart attack was in his immediate future if he didn't calm down. How on earth was he supposed to be calm? He had actually taken these nameless people up on their offer without being certain they had anything to offer him beyond a bullet in the brain.

He was desperate.

His sleep had been shitty after he'd taken the bus home, and even Zoe curling up on the bed with him hadn't helped. He'd given up at dawn and gone through the motions of feeding Zoe, drinking his morning portion of blood—and then another when his nerves refused to steady, and packing his bag. He'd spent the whole day with Riley after setting Stephen up as the designated cat-sitter, but all those hours hadn't really prepared him for this trip. Riley was depending on him, or so he had convinced himself, and the thought of going out of town and not coming back terrified him.

It might have been summer outside, balmy and warm, but the cab was arctic with the AC on full blast. Bastian dug into his backpack and pulled out Riley's favorite UT hoodie. It was oversized and worn to the point of having small holes along the seams of the sleeves, but it still smelled like Riley. Bastian clutched the ball of fabric and inhaled the scent before pulling it on over his shirt and jeans. When the cab jostled again, Bastian managed not to jump in his seat. He huddled into the corner, pulling the hood of the sweatshirt up over his head.

One way or another, he had to get through this. If he could get any information out of these people and return to Riley's side unharmed, then it would be worth it. Worst case scenario, he'd show up to a few really pissed off vampires and get killed. Bastian stiffened in his seat. He'd been trying to encourage himself, but the thought of it all ending over some stupid flyers he'd put up was just plain depressing. He tried to forget about the worst possibilities and focus on the best.

There was a chance the man who had called him was actually telling the truth. He'd made it sound like Bastian seeking help was understandable, and whoever had told him to call could have all the answers. That probably made the one at the top of the chain a vampire. No one else would be able to give him detailed information about the one who'd attacked him last year, much less answer the questions he had.

Bastian wasn't sure how he felt about coming face to face with a vampire other than the one who had turned him. He'd been ready to make demands of that vampire, but whoever was behind his sudden trip to Nashville obviously didn't respond well to demands or threats. Which left him with no options. Honestly, he was barely more than a kid out from under the thumb of his aunt and uncle. He didn't know what he was supposed to do. Hell, as they pulled up outside the very lavish hotel, Bastian had to admit he didn't even know what to *ask* another vampire. All the questions that had plagued him for so many months, even when he wasn't thinking about them, disappeared. In fact, the only question he could summon was *How can I save my lover?*.

"Sir?" The driver twisted around in the front seat. "Your fare has already been paid."

Bastian nodded, passing up a twenty dollar bill for a tip. "Thanks." He slid out of the car and looked up at the hotel. It really was posh. He took a deep breath of the humid air and forced his feet forward. There was no use in delaying the meeting. The sooner he met this mysterious vampire, the sooner he would have his answers and be back at Riley's side.

There was a greeter at the door, and the concierge looked him up and down disapprovingly until he gave his name and asked for the Presidential Suite. It was almost amusing to watch the arrogance slip behind a mask of hospitality. If he hadn't just been appraised like a side of beef first, the expression might have been convincing. He was escorted to the elevator, where the concierge swiped an access card for the top level before wishing him a nice visit and stepping back out of the elevator before the doors slid shut. Visitors didn't get key cards of their own. He should have expected that, but it made the whole visit feel more like a one-way ticket, and he shifted on his feet until the elevator chimed and opened on the top floor.

There was only one door in the small hallway outside the elevator, and Bastian took a deep breath and released it slowly before reaching for the knocker on the door. Before he could even touch it, the door swung open to reveal a middle-aged man in what had to be a custom suit and tie. It fit perfectly and somehow managed to look formal without appearing severe.

"Mr. Rossi." The instant the man spoke, Bastian knew it was the man from the phone. Anger spiked through him, making his back and shoulders prickle, but he forced a smile.

Half a dozen rude comments were on the tip of his tongue, but he swallowed them back and replied with a simple, "That's me."

"Please, come inside." The man stepped to the side and gestured him in with an elegant sweep of his hand. "My mistress has been awaiting your arrival. This way."

Bastian entered the suite, following the man into the dimly lit main room. It was a living room-dining room set up, but most of the furniture had been pushed out of the way. He was really surprised to see almost two dozen people scattered about, lounging on dozens of pillows, more than half of them undressed. Heat rose into Bastian's cheeks as he caught sight of a young woman on her knees, her body bowed back, her wrists caught by a broad, dark-skinned man behind her. Her eyes were covered with a silk tie, and she was gasping, writhing. His mouth was pressed to her throat, a small smear of blood evident to Bastian's eyes. Then he caught sight of a slim, almost boyish figure between the woman's thighs, and he realized another woman was going down on her as she was being fed from.

His eyes swept the room, but his other senses told him more. There were only perhaps six or seven humans here, and all the rest were vampires. Their eyes looked him over briefly, but their attention was drawn back to the warm, willing flesh passed around like a casserole at a potluck. Bastian was ashamed as his hunger flared, and the supple body of a tanned, athletic-looking man moved into his line of sight. He paused, closed his eyes, and let out a long breath. Riley was waiting for him, counting on him, and he needed his answered. Answers wouldn't be found in this hedonistic display.

Bastian picked up his pace until he was nearly stepping on the middle-aged man's heels. "Who's in charge?"

"I am." It was a woman's voice, deep and thick with a middle-eastern accent. His guide stopped outside a door, and even though Bastian knew the voice had come from within, they sounded as though the speaker were right beside him. The woman spoke again, her amused words floating easily to his ears and setting his heart racing. "Come now, sweet boy, you have come this far, what is another step?"

Bastian looked up at the man, but all he received was another of those infuriating smiles and a gesture toward the door. Swallowing thickly, he opened the door and stepped into a large bedroom. The decadence of the room's furnishings was only made more overwhelming by the addition of naked, aroused men posed here and there. It was distracting as hell, and his eyes darted around to them before settling on the woman in the center of the bed.

Bastian couldn't help but notice her height first. She was tall, even reclined against the pillows at the ornate headboard, and her legs seemed to go on for days in her leather boots that laced all the way up to mid-thigh. Her hair was long and thick, a wave to it so that it curled down around the corset she was wearing. Black hair and black leather. Bastian knew fetish gear was uncomfortable by default, but she lounged in it like it was the most comfortable set of pajamas she owned.

She was undeniably attractive—hell, sex appeal practically oozed from her—but there was a dangerous edge to the angles of her face that made Bastian hesitate to say or do anything beyond staring into her dark eyes. When the door clicked shut behind him, he jumped, the spell temporarily broken.

Her rich laughter filled the room, though he couldn't precisely say why. It shouldn't have. A laugh doesn't have the ability to worm its way into the small corners of a room, but this one did. She shifted on the bed, serpent-like, and Bastian couldn't help the way he took a step back. The woman's smile was feral and cold, her fangs glinting in the dim light. Bastian knew the lighting had been chosen to perfectly accentuate her skin and coloring, making her a piece of art for those lucky enough to be invited into the cobra's den.

His throat worked, trying to form words, but he was scared. Hell, he was terrified. Riley was dying, and here he was amidst the decadence of Sodom with the demon-queen Lilith beckoning him closer. "I need answers," he choked out.

"Answers?" She rose up onto her knees. "You don't even bring me a gift, and the first words out of your mouth are a demand." The woman made a tsking noise. "Shame on you."

"The guy who called me didn't say anything about a gift," Bastian all but sputtered in his panic. "He just said to come, so I came." Another of those strange laughs that surrounded him, and she inched closer to him. Bastian took yet another step back and ran into the closed door.

"I understand," she purred. "You're new. Young yet. You will learn. For now, I will give *you* a gift." She made a brief motion with her hand and a young man who could be no more than seventeen stepped forward and knelt. He bared his throat, already littered with old and new markings from fangs. "You look famished."

Hunger scratched at his stomach and throat, but when he moved to hug himself, Riley's sweatshirt rubbed against his arms. Riley was the last one he'd fed from, the only one he'd ever taken blood from directly. His eyes darted from the woman to the boy who was meant to be his meal. "Am I allowed to say 'Thanks, but no thanks'?"

Her eyes instantly narrowed on him, and Bastian wished he'd kept his mouth shut. "Is he not to your liking?" she asked, looking Bastian up and down as if she could read his preferences with a glance.

"No, he's fine. I just..." His voice trailed off. He didn't know how to explain it without embarrassing himself.

"You're shy?" She tittered behind long fingers. "Come now. It is poor manners to refuse an offered meal, and Seth has been looking forward to your visit all day."

Bastian glanced at the kneeling man again. "I have a boyfriend."

"So?" She tilted her head. "He's in a coma, and you are my guest."

A spark of anger lit brightly in his chest, and he had to clench his jaw tightly to keep from yelling at her. She spoke so casually about Riley, as if it made no difference that his lover was all but brain dead. Maybe Riley didn't matter to her, but he mattered to Bastian. "Riley's possessive. He wouldn't want me feeding from someone else."

"Such an attachment to that human," she sighed, a hint of annoyance in her eyes as she shifted on the bed. "He is not here and cannot be contacted, so your choices are to be polite and have your answers or leave with nothing."

Bastian opened his mouth to argue, but shut it again before he could make a huge mistake. Like it or not, she was right. He didn't want to betray Riley, but if he didn't get what he came for, being faithful wouldn't really matter.

His legs felt like they were made of Jell-O as he finally pushed away from the door and crossed to Seth. He knelt down and did his best to ignore the hot, pulsing allure of his throat as he reached out and righted Seth's face. "Do you consent to this?"

The woman laughed at him from her perch on the bed. "Of course he does!"

"Look, I don't even know what your name is yet, but Seth here is the one I'm about to bite, so I'd rather hear it from him, okay?" When she just rolled her eyes a bit, he turned his attention back to Seth. "Do you want me to drink from you?"

Bastian could sense more than see the flush that moved over Seth's cheeks in the low light, and it made that gnawing hunger inside return. Seth's eyes darted to his mistress, but he nodded, whispering, "Yes. I want this. I've waited." Bastian felt a shiver run through Seth's neck and shoulder. He could do little more than nod as he leaned forward, drawn in by the pulse that grew stronger and faster every passing second.

He made it as fast and painless as possible, letting instinct guide his fangs just deep enough for a light bleed. The blood that spilled into his mouth was hot and potent, and Bastian shuddered as he sucked on the wound. He drew a few large swallows from Seth with a muffled moan, and the rush of blood wiped out all thought of Riley and answers from his mind. It was the blood. Just the blood. It consumed him as he held Seth in a fast grip. He hadn't tasted anything this fresh and delicious in weeks, and the need to gorge was overwhelming until the mistress vampire's voice slithered in over the throb of Seth's heartbeat.

"Good boys," she drawled. Her encouragement pulled Bastian out of the moment, and he took a last tiny swallow before pulling away. He sat back on the thick pile floor, his eyes squeezed shut as he panted. Everything inside his body was telling him to go back, to take more blood, but he couldn't. He'd taken his taste, and that would have to be enough.

Her voice sounded in his ear. She was much closer now, behind him, but he didn't open his eyes. "You want more," she whispered. "Why not *take* it? Take him?" Seth was still in front of him, he could smell the young man, the blood a copper tang to his senses. "He wants it, and I know you do, too. I can scent the lust and hunger on you like three-day-old stink."

Bastian bit back a whimper and gripped at the rug with his hands until he knew he could speak without his voice wavering. It took just about as long to convince himself not to strike again. "I'm not here for Seth." Guilt knotted his stomach, soured the pleasure from the blood, and part of him was happy about it. The guilt gave him a little more control, and he steadied his breathing.

"How disappointing you are, Sebastian. All that wasted potential," she muttered, a creaking shift of leather signaling her movement back to the bed. Bastian looked at Seth when he opened his eyes, and only thoughts of Riley kept him from licking the small trail of blood off Seth's collarbone and chest. He wasn't sure what to do now, but luckily, he had a little help. "Pet him, Sebastian. Assure him he is good, that he has pleased you."

It meant getting closer again, but Bastian let out a slow exhale and scooted forward. He carded his fingers through Seth's blond hair over and over and hugged him close for a moment. "Thank you, Seth. You taste wonderful, and you've pleased both me and your mistress. My hesitance isn't your fault."

When he pulled back, Seth swayed a little drunkenly and smiled boyishly at him. "My pleasure, Sir," he slurred, his eyes dazed with pleasure.

"You may go now, Seth. Tell Todd to feed you well." Approval finally warmed the woman's voice a fraction, and Bastian watched as Seth crawled slowly past him and saw himself out, closing the door behind him.

The silence grew a bit awkward as Bastian rose to his feet, but he just didn't know what to say. He'd done what the other vampire wanted, and that would be enough, right?

"Was he truly that displeasing?" Her voice was cold again, as if that warmth he'd heard a minute before had just been his own mind playing tricks on him.

"He's just really young," Bastian couldn't help but comment, given the opportunity.

"He is a man by the standards of the world I grew up in."

Bastian didn't have a good response to that, so he just swallowed thickly, unconsciously savoring the last hints of blood in his mouth. "So, do I get your name now, or are you just waiting for me to call you Mistress?"

"You do not want to call me Mistress," she said as he patted the bedside. "Come. Sit."

Bastian glanced at the various men in the room, all still as statues. "I think you have enough company for your bed."

She smiled slowly, the expression dark and hungry. "They are not for conversation, but for eating. Come, Sebastian, and *sit*."

There was an unearthly power behind the command, and Bastian found himself sitting without another word. Then again, maybe it was just that fear compelled him to follow her directions. The last thing he wanted was to screw up now, when he was obviously so close to those answers he needed. He crossed his legs, sitting on the comforter just out of the other vampire's reach. "Can I please get your name now?" He tried to word it politely and save himself the embarrassment of being called out again on his fear.

"You are so preoccupied with names," she said. She slithered about on the bed a little until he was within reach of her. It took every ounce of control for him not to recoil when her finger trailed down his throat. It was warm, full of life stolen from those in this room. "You may call me Havva. It is what those not intimately familiar with me call me."

"Havva," he repeated, his voice tight. "I need answers."

Havva laughed, low and sensuous. "You need answers? No, sweet boy, you *want* answers. I have them. Novak was a poor creator, savaging you, turning you, and then leaving you behind to muddle about like a fish out of water."

Novak. Finally a name to go with the bastard who had turned his life upside down. Anger made the new blood in his system surge, and he clenched his fists in his lap. At least Havva thought Novak had done a shitty job, too. "Glad we agree on something," he ground out. "Would have saved me the effort of putting up those flyers if he'd just filled me in on the whole thing up front."

"That is not his way," Havva murmured, an artificial note of sympathy in her words. "You are but a single notch in a very long belt for Novak." She smiled, her finger teasing along his ear. "He likes the ones who struggle. The ones who struggle are usually given the most basic of instruction before he parts the following night."

"And the ones who don't struggle?"

"He tells them nothing. Some of them manage to work it out on their own. I am sure you have noticed that the change comes on us gradually. Still, there are always a few who cannot see the obvious when it is right in front of them. They do not usually make it more than three months."

Bastian fought not to cringe and pull away, but the muscles of his ear and neck twitched on instinct. "Great. So, now what? He inconveniences everyone including you. Isn't that a bad thing? You shouldn't have to pick up after his messes."

Havva clucked her tongue. "You will not succeed in making me angry with Novak. I find his antics amusing, and cleaning up after him is part of the fun."

"This is fun?" he asked, looking over his shoulder at her.

Havva's lips were very close to his, that sultry smile in place. "You think only of the comatose human, which means you cannot see the enjoyment in such a meeting. Todd tells me that your human is all but brain dead. A few more weeks and you would be rid of him." She sat back, reached out, and slid two fingers down the washboard stomach of the nearest man. The muscles shifted, but the man's face remained impassive. "But I can see the light of idiotic love in your eyes. You want to save him, no?"

"I wouldn't have come otherwise," Bastian admitted, letting her comment about love slide. "Is there a way?"

"You mean other than doing to him what was done to you?" At Bastian's nod, she sighed. "You could bond him to you. To some, it is a gift, a mark of honor, and to others, it is merely a half-life, a human kept around as a warm snack that can run errands."

"What would it mean for Riley? What exactly is this bond thing? If you mean my drinking from him, we were already doing that before the accident."

"And he has been desperate to feed you ever since?" Havva asked. This time, her smile wasn't one of dull amusement or seduction. It was knowing, and it sent a cold shiver down Bastian's spine.

"Yeah." Bastian's thoughts were suddenly caught in a whirlwind of memories, from the way Riley would pull him close and offer his neck every time they were intimate to the argument they'd had the afternoon before Riley was hurt. "I told him it was getting bad."

"Bad? Hardly!" Havva laughed. "It's one of our better tricks. It makes finding regular food all too easy."

"Riley isn't just food. He's my boyfriend and means a lot to me," Bastian snapped, ducking away from another of Havva's casual touches.

"Of course, or you would not have been able to start the bond with him by accident. It takes a certain intent if you do not feel emotionally attached to them. They become devoted, obsessed." Havva leaned back again to tease the nude man beside the bed. "So much easier to train and control."

For a moment, Bastian thought he'd be sick. It was wrong, forcing people into that crazed kind of devotion. Havva obviously saw it as some game, but it had never been a game to Bastian. He hadn't wanted to ensnare Riley. The half-bond had happened without him even trying. He wasn't sure if that was better or worse. Either way, it meant Riley hadn't had a choice, and that made Bastian a predator in ways he still wasn't comfortable with. "How do I complete the bond?"

"It is instinct. You know how to complete it."

Bastian flushed and looked away. She was right. Deep down, the answer rose up as bright as day. "Feed him from me," he whispered. "I have to let him feed from me."

Havva moaned softly. "Yes. And you will have to feed him for the rest of his life. If you don't," she purred, reaching out to snuff one of the candles with her fingers. "Humans are so delicate."

The thought made every inch of Bastian's skin crawl. "I'd take care of him. I'd always take care of him." He knew he was saying it more to reassure himself than anyone else. A thought occurred to him, though, and he had to ask, "What if he ends up... not wanting to be with me? Would it be a choice between me or death?"

"You are saving him from death. Those who are bonded to avoid death only do so through their master's good graces." Havva frowned, the expression odd on her face. "There is no way to cheat death and remain completely human. He is either your bonded or he is dead."

Bastian could feel the bile in the back of his throat. "What happens if he doesn't get fed?"

"Withdrawal, and then death," she said, and there was no arguing with her tone. "It would take two to three weeks for the bonded to revert to the original state, and that descent would not be a pleasant one."

The shock of being pulled from a coma just to be plunged back into one again would probably kill Riley. Bastian didn't have to be a doctor to know that much, and it made him shift uncomfortably in his seat. Saving Riley would mean taking all choice from him, forcing him into this new, dependent kind of life. He wasn't sure if Riley would thank him or hate him for it, which made his choice infinitely more difficult to make. "So I make him into a vampire, or I make him into a... what would you call it?"

"A ghoul, a day-walking servant. Vampires like you—the sentimental ones—sometimes call them their Bonded." Her lips quirked up into an amused expression at the last. What she found quaint, Bastian found romantic. If robbing your lover of their choice so you can have them with you forever could be called romantic instead of plain old selfish.

"I'll have to think about it," Bastian whispered, hugging himself in Riley's oversized sweatshirt.

Havva slid her hand up his back and threaded her fingers into his hair. "Time is ticking, but we both know what choice you will make. Once a week. You will need to feed him once a week. As he grows older, the need will become less acute, feeding able to be stretched sometimes up to a month before the need claws at them, but, for now, once a week."

Bastian wet his lips. "Once a week," he said with a nod. "If he wants more?"

A chuckle rumbled in her throat. "He will always want more."

Chapter Ten

Bastian paced the length of Riley's hospital room for what had to be the twentieth time. It was night, and he had closed the door to the room for a little privacy. The night shift nurses didn't seem to mind it much now that he'd been doing it on and off over the weeks Riley had been here. All the better now that Bastian had something a lot more shady to do away from prying eyes.

Havva had been right about one thing. He'd already made up his mind. It was selfish as hell, but he had to save Riley's life, even if it meant ultimately risking their relationship. Even so, he'd spent the last three nights at Riley's bedside, praying Riley would pull out of the coma on his own so he wouldn't have to go through with the bonding. He didn't want to rob Riley of choice, but, dammit, he didn't want to be left behind! He loved Riley. Bastian knew that in the deepest, darkest parts of his soul. Life without Riley wasn't an option.

Riley, though, had stubbornly been the same as when he'd left for Nashville: no change, no responses, no improvement in brain activity. Bastian had just sat and talked the whole thing out with Riley, telling him everything that had happened. Even if Riley couldn't hear or understand him, it made Bastian feel a little better just to share it. Just saying the words helped to make the situation real.

Time was running out. The last three days had done nothing but solidify the direction he'd take. If Riley had shown a sign of improvement, maybe he would have held off. The truth was, Riley wasn't getting any better. He had to face it. It was time for him to take matters into his own hands.

He wrung his hands as he paced, trying to rid himself of the jitters that had set in the moment he'd relieved Cheryl from her post at nightfall. He knew what he had to do. Havva had been very clear when he'd asked for a step-by-step from her. She might have been scary as hell, especially with the way she kept humans as pets, but Bastian had to admit she had been helpful.

"A quick bite, a sip from him, and then make him drink from you. You can do this," he tried to reassure himself. Havva had said it was all about intention, that Riley's body would somehow know the difference. As long as he stayed focused, it should work. If it didn't work, at least he had a contact number Havva had given him for a vampire in the area who could help if he really got in trouble. He was hoping he wouldn't have to ask any favors, though, not if most vampires were like her.

He turned on his heel at the end of the room, facing Riley's bed again, and the sight made him stop pacing. "You can do this," he repeated to himself, jumping in place a couple times like an athlete warming up for the main event. "No more stalling. Just do it. Just save him."

He nodded to himself and crossed to Riley, sitting on the edge of the bed. He wasn't completely sure how Riley would react to it all, but at the very least, he had to be able to get the blood down Riley's throat. The tracheal tube keeping Riley's airway open had to go, even if it put him at risk. At worst, he'd call in a nurse to put it back in if he failed. But he wouldn't fail. That's what he had to keep telling himself as he eased the tube out of Riley's throat as gently as possible.

Bastian's heart pounded in his chest, and he cradled Riley's face in his hand for a moment, kissing Riley's lips as he hadn't been able to do the last few weeks. He made quick work of turning off the machines the way he'd seen the nurses reset them from time to time. When he returned to Riley's side and bent down to kiss his throat, the hum of the machines had faded into silence. He could hear Riley's slow pulse, and he took a deep breath before exhaling slowly. He didn't dare wait any longer.

The strike was light, just enough power behind his fangs to break Riley's fragile skin, and he moaned softly at the familiar taste of Riley's blood as a few drops oozed onto his tongue. He hadn't fully realized how much he had missed Riley's flavor. Even Seth's blood hadn't compared. He had to force himself not to suck at the shallow wound, to bend all his thought on making his half of the bond as he licked the traces of blood from his bite.

When he was certain he'd had at least a mouthful of Riley's blood, he pulled back and brought his wrist to his mouth. It stung when he scraped his fang over the skin. He immediately transferred his wrist to Riley's mouth, holding Riley's lips and jaw open a little awkwardly. It was a bit messier than he'd thought, and he cursed under his breath, wishing he had a few more hands to help out.

"It'll be all right," he breathed, talking to himself as much as to Riley. "This bond will make you mine, and I'll take care of you. I promise I'll take care of you." He kept his wrist against Riley's lips as his other hand massaged Riley's

S.L. Armstrong & K. Piet

throat, trying to get him to swallow. "C'mon, Riley. Drink. It'll all be okay if you just drink and wake up." It felt like an eternity before the muscles beneath his massaging hand finally contracted, and he breathed a small sigh of relief before working the muscles for another swallow, and then a third. He focused, every thought encouraging Riley to bond with him, making promises he'd do everything in his power to keep.

Doubt started to creep in after a couple minutes, but he clenched his jaw. He couldn't give up. Riley was depending on him. If this was his only chance, he wasn't going to half-ass it and screw up. A need sparked inside him, not just the need to keep feeding Riley his blood, but a deeper need to just keep him alive. With every beat of his frantic heart, that need became stronger, and his brow creased with worry. "Please," he whispered, his eyes searching Riley's face for any change, any movement beneath the closed eyelids. "Please, come back to me."

Riley's sudden gasp for breath made Bastian jump and snatch his hand back from Riley's mouth on instinct. An instant later, he could hear Riley's heartbeat surge, louder and stronger than it had been in months. Relief was a blast of warmth through Bastian's body, and his arms trembled as he supported Riley's head. A weak cough wracked Riley's withered body. It was the first movement he'd seen out of Riley since he'd first arrived at the hospital. For that moment, Riley coughing was the most beautiful sound on the planet.

Riley's eyelids fluttered, and even though the eyes didn't open, Bastian's heart soared. A rough mumble escaped Riley, and Bastian leaned down. "What? What did you say?" he asked, unable to keep the tremor out of his voice.

"Eggs... or wa-" Riley coughed again and licked his lips. "Waffles for... breakfast..."

Bastian frowned for a moment, fear lurking at the edges of the joy in his mind. What was Riley talking about? Eggs or waffles? A smile broke out on his face when he placed the question. That's what Riley had asked him before bed the night before the day of the accident. He felt tears sting at his eyes as he hugged Riley to him.

"Waffles," he choked out, kissing Riley's hair. "Waffles whenever you want them from now on."

Riley blinked several times, confusion furrowing the pale brow. "Where am I?" he asked, his voice rasping out.

"In the hospital." Bastian heard footsteps coming down the hall. He eased Riley back down on the bed and rushed into the bathroom, wetting a washcloth there. "You were in an accident," he explained, returning to Riley's side. "You've been in a coma."

"What?" Riley tried to bat his hands away, but Bastian was insistent. He had to get the blood off Riley before the damn nurse burst in. "Accident?"

"I'll explain in a minute, but, Riley, you need to hold still. They can't see all this blood—"

Riley swatted at him again just as the door swung open, and Riley shoved the bloody washcloth into the sleeve of his shirt. He turned to face the nurse, revealing Riley's alert, if baffled, face. "He woke up!" Bastian crowed.

The nurse frowned, looking around at the silent machines. "I'll go fetch the on call doctor," she mumbled.

"You shouldn't have shut off the machines or removed his tube."

Bastian affected his most contrite expression. "I'm sorry. It won't happen again. He was just struggling, and my first thought was to make him comfortable."

"Don't touch anything," she said, and turned sharply on her heel.

Bastian looked down at Riley and smiled. "She may think I'm crazy, but at least you're awake."

Riley's eyes panned the room, and then slowly rose. They stared at one another as the cobwebs were swept aside in Riley's brain. Finally, Riley whispered, "What did you do?"

"What I had to," Bastian breathed, eyes darting back to the door. More footsteps, and he took Riley's hand and squeezed. Riley didn't squeeze back. He clenched his jaw as the door swung open again. "I did what I had to."

Riley

Chapter Eleven

Riley stared out the window of the cab as they drove through the nearly silent city streets. It was after one in the morning. The hospital had been left behind, Bastian insisting they leave as soon as possible. The doctors had wanted to keep him, but Bastian was agitated. Riley didn't know what was going on, but he knew Bastian had done something he probably shouldn't have.

The silence stretched between them, uncomfortable and thick. Everything was strange. It was as if he were a stranger in his own body, and Riley couldn't quite put his finger on why. He shifted in the backseat, his muscles tired and sore. The doctor—what had been the doctor's name?— had told him to take it easy. If Riley wasn't going to stay in the hospital for observation and rehabilitation, then Bastian should take things slowly with him. Rehabilitation? What rehabilitation had he needed? He wasn't some gibbering idiot. He could walk and talk and eat. Riley wasn't pissing himself, after all. The confusion made his head hurt.

They came to a stop at the walk that led to the converted colonial they called home. Riley stared at the building blankly, but he couldn't muster up any excitement. It was home, right? His cat was in there. Sweet little Zoe, who probably missed him like crazy. All his things were in there. His life was in that quaint two-bedroom, one-bath apartment that he'd accepted Bastian into. Still, Riley sat there, staring through the windshield spotted with water as a summer storm finally broke over them. It was home, yes, but it was also alien.

Just like you.

The thought crept through Riley's mind. He shivered. He didn't like that thought. He was Riley, a college student struggling to become a vet. He'd had an accident. Now, he needed to pick his life back up and move forward. No more thoughts about being the same but different. Once they were inside, he could demand Bastian come clean with him, but right now, he just wanted to feel like himself again.

"Come on," Riley croaked. "Let's get inside."

Bastian looked at him uncertainly, but then nodded, paying the driver quietly. Riley opened the door and stepped out into the downpour, the rain warm from the summer heat. It felt good, refreshing and cleansing. It gave Riley hope that, whatever had happened, this was a fresh start. The accident had meant something. It had been a wake-up call to both Bastian and him.

"Riley!" Bastian gave his arm a tug. "You're soaking wet. We need to get inside."

Riley followed Bastian up the walk and into the apartment. It was dark, only the quiet hum of the air conditioner unit in the bedroom breaking the eerie silence. Riley stood in the living room, dripping onto the hardwood floors, and nearly jumped when the refrigerator kicked on. It was as loud as a rocket! He heard the soft sweep of Zoe's tail, and then the thunderous thump of her paws hitting the floor as she left the bed and came to the living room. His heart hammered in his chest and he stared at Bastian.

The only question that would form on his lips was the same one he'd asked the previous night before the doctors and his family had descended. "What did you do?"

Bastian turned from hanging up his coat, his hands held out as if to calm Riley down. "Don't freak out. It's gonna be all right."

He heard Bastian's heartbeat as Bastian slowly stepped closer, and he took a step back to keep out of reach. Zoe's happy meow startled him, and he yelped, his hands instinctively going to his ears, shielding them from all the noise. "What did you do?" he asked more frantically, unable to do anything but match Bastian's steps. The arm of the sofa hindered his retreat. He gripped the fabric behind him, resisting the urge to side-step the sofa and run. But run where? There was nowhere to run in their small apartment.

"Riley!" Bastian had been calling his name, but he'd barely noticed with both their pulses thundering in his ears. "Try to calm down. Short story is that I found other vampires and they taught me a way to save you. I'll explain, but you need to breathe and get out of your wet clothes before you make yourself sick."

Riley shook his head, glaring at Bastian. "You changed me. You did something and now I hear things I shouldn't." His voice gained in volume until he was shouting at Bastian. "What the hell did you do!"

"I gave you my blood and made you into my Bonded." Bastian shifted on his feet. "You're not a vampire, but kinda like a ghoul. The bond was halfway there already. That's why you were so desperate to feed me all the time. You have to always drink from me now, but you're awake again. The doc said the longer you were in that coma, the less chance there was of you ever coming back. I did what I had to so you wouldn't die!"

"You..." Riley swallowed, and he thought he could taste the remnants of copper in the back of his throat. It was impossible, though. He'd had food and water since Bastian had woken him. Bastian had changed him, turned him into something not quite human and not quite vampire. Anger rose in him, hot and bitter. "You *bastard*!"

Bastian blinked in surprise. "Riley—"

"No!" Riley grabbed tightly to his anger. It gave him confidence, strength, and he shoved Bastian. "You didn't even *ask* me! No. I won't drink anymore. If I want this... bond... then we'll do it when *I'm* ready, not when *you* decide I'm ready."

"You'll die!" Bastian's voice wavered, and he could see the panic in Bastian's eyes. "If we'd done this while you were awake and healthy, things would've been different, but you were in a fucking coma. If you don't drink from me, you go back to the way you were. The shock of it would kill you!"

Riley clenched his teeth. "So I'm stuck like this. Chained to you forever. *Beholden*, kept like a pet!"

Bastian winced. "Please don't say it like that. You make it sound like it's a fate worse than death. We were already committed to one another. This just sorta makes it more permanent. I thought—"

"What, that I would be happy you didn't give me a choice?" Riley snapped.

"There wasn't any choice," Bastian ground out, anger narrowing his eyes. "Life or death. Make a blood bond with you or watch you flatline after another week in the hospital."

Riley shivered and hugged himself. "You did something that can never be undone. You made it so my life absolutely depends on you." Sorrow and hopelessness welled inside him. "You've taken away my independence, Sebastian."

The anger drained from Bastian, and his lover seemed to wilt before his eyes. "I gave you life at a cost. I thought it was one you'd willingly pay." Bastian's arms dropped to his sides. "I promised to take care of you. Right now, that means getting you into a warm shower. It'll help with the sensitivity."

After a moment, Riley nodded. A hot shower would help. He was filthy from weeks in a hospital bed. "All right," he muttered. He needed time. "But this discussion is *not* over." A little time, a hot shower, a solid meal, and Riley thought he would be able to piece it all together and make some sort of decision. What that decision would—*could*— be, he didn't know, but there was one for him to make.

Bastian led him into the bathroom and stripped him, all the while murmuring about how he couldn't live without Riley, that he loved Riley, would have done anything to save him.

Had done anything to save him.

Every word rang in his ears, the whispers as loud as a church bell. Bastian's words were deafening in their softness, and he finally closed his eyes and shoved his head under the rush of the shower head. It was silence here. No more words. No more sounds. It was just the rush of water and the quiet of steam. Bastian left him alone, promising a meal, Riley thought.

In the nightlight-lit bathroom, Riley stared at the tile wall. It was brilliant white even in the low light, and then the grout lines blurred. He was thankful the water hid the tears that rolled down his face, even with no one else to see. Everything had changed, and Riley closed his eyes against the truth of it all. What was he supposed to do now?

The air conditioner hummed back to life and startled Riley. He twitched on the bed, trapped between Bastian's body and Zoe's. Zoe had been attached to him from the moment he came out of the shower, scattering only once when he'd yelled at Bastian again. He swallowed as he stared up at the ceiling, and the coppery tang of blood lingered on the back of his tongue. His eyes darted to the clock beside the bed. Three in the morning. He'd pressed his mouth to a wound on Bastian's throat six hours ago, and he could still taste the blood.

He closed his eyes. His chest tightened with emotion, and he thought he might begin to cry again. Was this going to be their eternity? Bitterness, resentment, and fights about a choice that couldn't be changed? That wasn't a future. It was a cheesy, depressing soap opera just waiting to happen, and Riley didn't want that. Hell, he didn't want any of this. He'd just wanted a veterinary practice, a husband, a lot of pets, a nice house with some land, and, just maybe, a kid. It was the American dream, right?

Now, that dream was smashed into a million pieces, and Riley knew they could never put it back together. Bastian was a vampire, and now he was that vampire's fucking ghoul. Ghoul. The word was horrific. Bastian had also called him his Bonded. Bonded was nicer. It had a gothic, romantic ring to it that might look great splashed across the pages of some 1970s bodice ripper. Whatever the word, it was a shackle around his throat. He couldn't stop any of it. Once a week, he had to drink from Bastian. From what he understood, he'd want to drink from him... and to have Bastian feed from him, too. The perfect symbiotic relationship. His vet-mind could appreciate it. The vampire keeps the ghoul alive, healthy and young and able-bodied, while the ghoul feeds the vampire and does his dirty work during the day.

Riley didn't like it. He didn't like it one bit. The anger bubbled up again, and he realized he was grinding his teeth. He exhaled slowly, softly, and tried to think about it all rationally. The air conditioner kicked off again, and the house was silent, leaving him alone with his dark thoughts. Bastian had done what he'd thought necessary, and while he'd saved Riley's life, Riley thought if given a little more time, his body would have healed. He would have woken up human and unbound, if only Bastian had waited.

If he had waited, you'd be dead. That damned voice whispering at him again. Riley didn't care if the logical part of his brain knew Bastian had done the right thing. It was the principle of the matter. What happened next time when Bastian got it into his head that he knew better than Riley?

What happened when Bastian didn't want Riley anymore?

That was the heart of the matter. That was what kept nagging at Riley. What would happen when Bastian decided there were better men for him? The choices then would be to drag Riley around like an anchor, make him into a vampire, or just... let him die. Riley didn't like any of those options. The equality of their relationship had been compromised. He'd lost his independence and his equality in one selfish and selfless move.

Because wasn't Bastian as trapped as he was?

Bastian rolled over in bed with a sigh, his arm finally lifting up off Riley. Riley closed his eyes and tried to fall back asleep, but the anger swelled up again and all he wanted to do was run. The cage, no matter how intangible it seemed, was still a cage. Jake had put him in a cage. In that cage, Jake had been able to twist him around. When someone else held the key to that cage, they had all the fucking power, and he had *nothing*. Impotent rage and directionless fear, that's all he had, and both warred in him again as the gentle rasp of Zoe snoring blared in his ears. He couldn't think here. Not in this apartment with this man. He needed some time. Adjustment. That's what he needed. Just a little time away to adjust. Maybe the vampire Bastian had spoken to had lied. Maybe, if he let Bastian's blood run its course through him, he could revert back to who and what he was before the accident.

Carefully, Riley slipped from the bed, giving Zoe a small scritch as she settled down in the warm spot he'd left behind. He didn't want to leave her, but he didn't know where the hell he was going yet. Maybe to Cheryl's. Cheryl was safe. A safe place. He'd start there.

As quietly as possible, Riley dressed and stuffed a duffle pack full of clothes. He could buy the necessities at a Wal-Mart on the way to Cheryl's. Right now, he just needed clothes. Riley shoved his feet into some sneakers, grabbed his wallet, keys, and cellphone, and then let himself out of the apartment. Once at the street, he called the local cab company, gave them his credit card number, and the hung up and waited.

He glanced back at the house, the night loud around him, and he wondered if he would ever be back. His heart ached at the thought of never seeing Bastian or Zoe again, but then the rustle of leaves, as loud as a fucking Mack truck, brought him back to reality. He had to know if he could do this on his own, and he couldn't learn that with Bastian shoving blood at him every couple of days.

The cab pulled up and Riley slid inside. He gave him Cheryl's address and surprised himself by not looking back at the house as the cab pulled away. When they were halfway to Cheryl's, he took out his cellphone and sent a text message to Bastian's phone.

Don't try to find me. I'll call you when I'm ready.

Chapter Twelve

The end of summer was a blur. Riley couldn't remember what day it was, actually. The first four or five days at Cheryl's, away from Bastian, had been fine. He'd done pretty damn well, in fact. There had only been the one bout of crying after he'd shown up on her doorstep, but Cheryl hadn't held it against him. She'd told him tragedies like his accident changed people, and that if Bastian really loved him, he'd give him the space he needed to find himself.

Riley had settled into a routine. It'd been easy, really. Only three calls from Bastian. One to his cell and two to Cheryl's landline. Cheryl had talked to Bastian the second time, and the calls had stopped. Riley hadn't understood his momentary disappointment, thinking Bastian had given up on him so easily, but then he had to get his head on straight. Bastian hadn't given up on him, only shown respect. Yes, it had been respect.

And so the days had passed. He'd signed up for his fall classes, gone out with Cheryl and Matt, and he'd even managed to get the bookstore to order his books. After a week, though, he'd grown restless. Cheryl had asked him what was wrong because he looked like he was ready to claw his own skin. It was pretty close to what he wanted to do. There was a nagging feeling in the back of his mind that he needed to be somewhere. He was tired, he told himself, and he'd gone to bed early.

The next day was worse. Riley was ravenous. He'd eaten almost everything in Cheryl's small, woefully understocked kitchen, and then ordered $100 worth of takeout. He was also horny. Incredibly, uncomfortably horny. His mind kept drifting to thoughts of Bastian. Of his cock, his mouth, those incredible hands... He was hard all the time, starving, and plagued by thoughts of his boyfriend. This, he decided, wasn't the way things should be. When Stephen invited him to a party at his frat house, Riley had jumped at the opportunity. Dancing, a little drinking, plenty of food, he thought it would take his mind off sex and Bastian and the skin-crawling need for *something* his body craved but wasn't getting.

That had been four days ago. Riley rolled over in the bed he currently occupied and blinked at the man beside him. Jeremy? John? Kevin? He couldn't remember the guy's name, but he did remember the amazing, two hour long marathon of sex they'd had the night before. Hell, his ass still hurt. He frowned, a wave of guilt washing over him. This wasn't like him. He'd been fucking a string of men since Stephen's party. He couldn't remember their names or even how many there had been.

He groaned, his cock hard against the come-stained bed. It didn't matter that he couldn't remember the guy's name. What he wanted was to wake him up, lube his cock, and ride him until they both came screaming. Again. And again. And again. He kissed his way up the guy's chest, nipping playfully at a nipple, and rubbed himself against a thick, toned thigh. The guy's eyes opened, revealing clear, bright blue eyes, and Riley slid his hand down the guy's stomach until he palmed his cock.

"Good afternoon," he purred. He was starving... so thirsty... and, God, his body ached for sex. He vaguely wondered if his one-night stand had a buddy who might be interested in joining them. "Sleep well?"

The guy gave him a sleepy smile. "Yeah. You fucked the shit out of me last night."

Riley reached for a condom and the lube as he rose up to his knees. "Mmm, I think I might fuck the shit out of you this morning, too."

The guy—Dean, that was his name—Dean rubbed his hands over Riley's thighs and hips. "You think so?"

"I know so." Riley rolled the condom down Dean's lovely cock, stroked some lube onto the latex, and straddled him. There wasn't any foreplay, any ounce of romance as he mounted the man, sliding down the thick shaft with a groan. As full and stretched as he was, it wasn't enough. It never felt like enough!

Dean groaned beneath him and groped his ass before thrusting up. It felt good, even with how sore his ass was, and he eagerly pushed back into every movement. It was just sex, nothing but a selfish taking of what he needed. Days and nights filled with sex, but it wasn't satisfying. Closing his hand around his own cock, Riley moaned and tried to push away the thought.

Fingers plucked at his nipples, distracting him, and he closed his eyes as he rode Dean hard. If he could just get off again, maybe the hunger that stung at his throat would go away. Maybe the thirst could be quenched with more alcohol. But every thrust, every cry Dean coaxed from him, just made the ache worse. Behind his closed eyelids,

Bastian's face hovered, beckoning him, and Riley shook his head trying to erase the vision.

When climax came, it was empty. Dean rolled over and fell back asleep, but Riley was restless. He needed *more*. Anything more. He got dressed in his rumpled clothes, picked up the bottle of vodka he'd dropped last night, and headed downstairs. Someone had to be around that could scratch his itch.

Riley was draped over a toilet. Whose toilet? He couldn't remember anymore. Another dry heave wracked his body, and he clung to the cool porcelain of the commode. Where was Matt? Or was it Stephen he'd come with? Maybe it was Lee... or Gary... or... fuck, how many guys had he run through since that first party? How long had he been away from Bastian? When was the last time he'd checked in with Cheryl?

The next heave brought up the remaining food he'd managed to eat an hour ago, and with it most of the booze. He flushed the toilet and leaned back against the shower stall door, running his hands through his greasy hair. Sweat dripped down his face, and he was sure he was about to pass out. Riley wondered if this was how a coke addict felt when they couldn't get a fix. He laughed, the sound high and crazed, and he looked around the small bathroom through tears. Where the fuck was he?

He shivered, cold right to the bone, even if he was sweating. Riley never felt warm anymore, and he scrubbed at his eyes. Nausea rolled through him, but all he did was hiccup. Hiccups he could deal with. His head was pounding. He was starving. As much as he wanted to eat, drink, he didn't think he could. He'd thrown up for the last full day... was it a day? Maybe two? God, what time was it?

The door opened a crack and a man with dark hair and round glasses peered inside. "You okay?"

Riley closed his eyes. "Just feeling a little under the weather," he murmured.

"You look like shit." The man let himself into the bathroom and turned on the shower. "Jason went to work. He asked me to look in on you."

"Jason," Riley echoed. Who was Jason? Which one was Jason? "That's thoughtful of him." He opened his eyes and took in the sight of the man. He was tall. Lean. That was all he saw, all he seemed to care about. The guy looked healthy, awake and alert. He smiled slowly. "And thoughtful of you, too. You planning on washing me?"

The guy laughed. "You don't even know me."

Riley tried to get to his feet. It took two attempts before he just remained on the floor. His head spun, throbbed with the sound of the man's heartbeat. "I could. What's your name?"

"Andrew." Andrew crouched in front of him as the room began to fill with steam. "And I know you're Sebastian's boyfriend, so I have no intention of fucking you. He's my friend, and I won't hurt him like you are."

Anger stabbed at Riley. He glared at Andrew. "Who the fuck asked you?"

Andrew smiled serenely. "You did with that come hither look of yours. What you don't seem to get is it doesn't work when you look like death barely warmed up."

Riley's eyes had been focused on Andrew's lips as they moved. When Andrew stopped talking, Riley was startled that he was actually staring at Andrew's throat. He met the soft, brown eyes. "Bastian screwed up."

"Maybe he did," Andrew said, "and maybe he didn't. I don't know. He doesn't talk about his personal life too much. What I do know is that if my boyfriend had just spent the last two weeks hopping on every available cock on campus, I wouldn't be waiting at home for him to come back."

"Two weeks?" Riley furrowed his brow as guilt twisted his stomach. Had he been away from Bastian for almost three weeks? He had thought a week, maybe. Get his head sorted, decide how he would deal with the changes... "That's not... not possible."

Andrew began to undress him. "It's the truth. You're a mess. God, you smell like you haven't bathed in weeks."

A bitter laugh rasped past his lips, and his eyes were again drawn to Andrew's throat. "I haven't. I didn't want a shower."

"You wanted cock."

Riley closed his eyes again. He was naked, and Andrew hoisted him up and sat him in the shower. The water was hot, but it didn't rid him of the chill. He couldn't stop shivering. "No, not cock," he said, leaning his head against the cool tile. "I needed... something..."

Andrew shook his head and crossed his arms. "Do you want me to call Sebastian?"

After a moment, Riley was hit by a moment of clarity. He looked up at Andrew as the puzzle pieces fell into place. "I needed Bastian," he said. Whenever he closed his eyes, it was Bastian he saw. Whenever he fucked someone, it was Bastian he wanted. And now, with Andrew, he was thinking of blood, but it wasn't Andrew's blood he wanted. "Please, call Bastian."

Chapter Thirteen

The drive was miraculously quiet. Riley had simply slumped in the front passenger seat beside Andrew. The lights flew past, almost hypnotic, and Riley thought about Bastian. If he were Bastian, he wouldn't take him back. He'd left Jake for far less an infraction. He'd fucked around. Bastian had risked his life going to see the other vampires, and then risked everything else to create the bond they now shared. Bastian had saved him, and in return, Riley had thrown a hysterical fit and walked out.

Shame washed through him. The crazed need he'd felt for the last two weeks had mysteriously vanished the moment Andrew had offered to call Bastian. He'd weakly washed and dressed before being ushered out to the car. Bastian was waiting for him. Riley knew this. Bastian had been waiting, worrying, and something inside him also knew that Bastian had been just as crazed as him. But, he was sure Bastian hadn't gone to the lengths he had in order to ease the symptoms.

That's what they were. With his mind clearer, Riley's medical mind had kicked into high gear. They had been symptoms of withdrawal, and now he was certain the pain and exhaustion he was experiencing was how a terminal patient must feel at the end. It was all his fault. Bastian had the answers, and he'd turned his back on him. Riley had been so stupid, rash and angry over the wrong things. He was still berating himself when the car came to a stop and Andrew shut off the engine.

"Do you need help?" Andrew murmured.

Riley pushed up from where he was leaning against the door and unfastened his seatbelt. He shook his head. "No." He smiled weakly at Andrew. It wasn't really a smile, he supposed, but more a grimace. His face was stiff, like a mask, and he gave up on the smiling. "Thank you. I'll tell Bastian to call you."

He opened the door and stepped out. He was on his own two feet and the door to his apartment looked a dozen miles away. For a moment, he considered asking Andrew for a hand to the door, but he quickly dismissed it. No, this was his responsibility. He'd let himself go so long, stupidly running from the most important thing in his life, and he would return to Bastian on his own two feet. He shut the door to the car and shoved off, his knees weak and unhappy.

One foot in front of the other. He kept thinking all he needed to do was put one foot in front of the other. One step at a time, and he came closer and closer to the door. By the time he reached his apartment, he was sweating, panting, and thought he just might pass out. He leaned against the door and turned the knob, but it was locked... and he'd left his keys at Cheryl's. A sob welled in his throat, and he thumped his fist against the door.

"Bastian?" Was that his voice? That gruff, rough sound? Could Bastian even hear him? "Bastian..."

The door suddenly gave way under his weight, and he toppled forward, unable to catch himself on the door frame. He closed his eyes, expecting to impact the wood floor inside the door. What he hit instead was softer, and he held on tightly as Bastian's arms closed around him and tugged him inside.

"Riley!" Bastian's voice was frantic with worry, and it just made his chest hurt. Bastian's heart was pounding under his ear, and it made his gut ache and his throat itch. "Can you stand? Shit, you can't die on me now!"

Thought was slow to come to him, slower than sensation. He felt the couch. He felt Bastian's shirt. He felt the smooth coolness of Bastian's skin. He felt desperate fingers moving over his body. What he couldn't do was pull his mind together long enough to form coherent words. No, he couldn't stand. Yes, maybe he was dying. If he was, it was his own damned fault.

His tongue felt dry and bloated in his mouth, and fear was like ice in his veins. Had he waited too long? Was there no fixing this? No going back? Riley forced his tongue to move, his lips to form words, and his throat to issue sound. "Bastian." It was the only word that mattered. Bastian must have righted him because his lips, as he tried to utter more words, were pressed to a pale throat.

Instinct kicked in, and Riley groaned. It was Bastian's throat. Under the thin, cream-colored skin flowed warmth, life, everything Riley craved. It wasn't borrowed life. It wasn't a chain to strangle him with. It was a gift. Bastian had gifted him with life, good health, and time. He'd been ungrateful, shunning that gift, and yet, here Bastian was, offering it again. No hesitation, no begging, it was just there, waiting.

"Bite," Bastian murmured. "Please, Riley, just bite."

A burning need flared inside his core and spread quickly to his throat and jaw. He didn't have to think. His muscles obeyed Bastian, pressing his mouth closer. He didn't have to search to find where Bastian's pulse beat strong. His body knew where to center on, and he didn't second guess the instinct. There was no warm up, no kisses or teasing with his tongue. His jaw opened, and then slammed back shut once more, his teeth cutting viciously into tender skin. Bastian stilled for a split second under him, and then every other sensation was lost to the gush of blood over his tongue.

The rush of heat nearly stole his breath away, and he moaned wetly before swallowing. The warmth spread down into him, true warmth, everything he'd been searching for the last two weeks. Bastian's arms tightened around him, urging him on, and Riley didn't second guess himself. He sucked fiercely at Bastian's throat, swallow after swallow, until he was gnawing at the wound, deepening it. He rocked on Bastian's lap—he was astride Bastian's lap, yes, he could feel that now—and his hands clawed at Bastian's shirt. Hungry instinct merged with burning arousal, desire hotter inside him now than it had been any other time since he'd woken in that hospital. Maybe it was even hotter than before the accident, before this change in him, because his cock was painfully hard, his pulse pounding through him with startling swiftness.

He thought his heart would burst. He loved Bastian, loved him even more now, and he groaned against his throat, another shudder wracking his body. Closer, he wanted, no, *needed*, to be closer, and the clothing between them hindered that. Riley released Bastian's throat only long enough to rip the shirt away in his impatience, Bastian's hands helping him out of his own. As soon as that was done, he struck again, latching onto Bastian's throat and wringing another cry from his lover as they pressed closer. Hands roamed, reacquainted themselves with bodies hungry for touch, and Riley drank, lost in a haze of lust, relief, and mind-numbing ecstasy.

"Fuck yeah. Drink me down," Bastian groaned, every sound vibrating against Riley's mouth. The raw need in Bastian's voice pulled another moan from his throat between swallows. Bastian bucked beneath him, and Riley ground down. A minute ago, every movement would have been a trial, but now, the blood moved through him, easing every ache, every hunger pang, every hint of death that had been creeping up on him.

His skin was on fire, overheating with every throb of his pulse, but the blood kept flowing, and he drank until Bastian pulled sharply on his hair. He was forced back with a cry, and for a moment, he struggled against Bastian, his mouth reaching for the trickle of blood. Only Bastian's possessive kiss stopped him from returning to the wound, distracting him enough to break the pull of instinct. He was full. In fact, he was almost bloated with Bastian's blood. The need inside him had been sated. Bastian knew it, knew when to stop him and take control.

He was suddenly drowning in Bastian's kisses. It was impossible not to give in. This was what he had needed most. This was what had been missing the last two weeks— not just the blood, but the love between them. He could taste it in the metallic tang, feel it in every swipe of Bastian's tongue and the bruising grip of Bastian's hands at his hips. Riley curled his tongue up along one of Bastian's fangs and scratched his nails over Bastian's nipples.

Bastian jerked back with a needy cry that rang in Riley's ears, and his lips curled up into a smile before Bastian claimed his mouth again. They panted between kisses, their fingers fumbling with the button and zipper of Riley's jeans. Lights danced on the edges of Riley's vision, and he finally abandoned Bastian's mouth, bending down to take a nipple between his lips. He sucked and pulled at it with his teeth, squirming as cool hands pushed denim aside and worked him free of his boxers.

His own hands made short work of Bastian's pajama bottoms, pushing them down as he shoved his hand between fabric and flesh. A shiver ran down his spine as he squeezed Bastian, savored the weight and girth of him. He was crazed, wanting to feel everything, Bastian's blood burning through him. As much as he wanted to thrust and stroke, make them both come, there was something holding him back, telling him he wasn't done. *They* weren't done. He scraped his teeth over Bastian's nipple, and then pulled up, bringing his eyes level with Bastian's. The need he felt was reflected there in dark eyes. Nothing was hidden from him, and he hid nothing in return.

Slowly, deliberately, he slid his thumb over the wet tip of Bastian's cock while tilting his head, exposing his throat to Bastian. Bastian had fed him, given him what he had denied he'd needed, and now he would give back. That new, silent knowledge he'd gained the moment his lips had sealed over Bastian's throat told him it was a give and take between them. Bastian would keep him alive now, keep him healthy, love him, protect him from any harm. But Riley would keep Bastian, too. Keep him warm, flushed, laughing. He would love Bastian as much as Bastian loved him, and they would make it work. All he had to do was embrace their new life together.

Riley swallowed, his hand moving up and down Bastian's cock, matching the rhythm Bastian set on his own. "My blood is yours," he whispered, offering himself completely.

Unrestrained hunger flashed in Bastian's hazel eyes, and a moment later, Bastian's fangs sank into his neck. The pain brought a ragged cry from his throat, but it disappeared almost as quickly as it had flared. Whatever power was in their bond, it turned the pain of Bastian's bite into pleasure, thick, sweet, and utterly addictive. It was Bastian's bite that had clouded his judgment months ago, made it so difficult to think of anything else, but they had been missing the other half. With Bastian's blood coursing through him, giving back now made everything fall into place.

Bastian's hand sped up on his cock, and all Riley could do was squirm and moan. The pleasure made his mind stall, his hand faltering in its pace on Bastian's shaft. He was sensitive, far more sensitive to Bastian's touch. It was like the last two weeks hadn't happened at all, like he hadn't come for months. The pressure built with such fierce intensity that he was helpless when it swelled and overtook him. His whole body bucked as pleasure—sharp as lightning—crashed into him, and he screamed, coming thickly over Bastian's fist.

By the time he came back to himself, he'd sagged against Bastian, twitching in the aftermath of one of the best damn orgasms he'd ever had. His eyes fluttered open, and that was when he realized Bastian had stopped feeding from him. Dark, hazel eyes stared down at him with an intensity that made Riley's heart ache. Unbidden, tears stung his eyes, and he choked out, "I'm sorry. I'm so sorry, Bastian. I love you. I promise I'll make it up... I promise. I'm just... so sorry." He pressed his brow to Bastian's shoulder and tried not to sob like a child.

"Riley," Bastian panted against his hair. Strong arms closed around him, holding their warm bodies even closer. "Oh, Riley... Shh..."

Bastian tried to soothe him without words, but the shift of Bastian's hips under him brought Riley's attention lower. It was probably uncontrollable, but Bastian was still hot and hard between them. It was an opportunity to act, to make good on his promise right away. One act couldn't possibly make up for everything that had happened in the last two weeks, but it was a start. He gathered together his renewed strength and straightened before sliding down between Bastian's parted legs.

He glanced up once at Bastian, and then pulled the pajama bottoms lower. Riley took in the sight of Bastian, the smell of his musk, and his mouth watered. He wrapped his fingers around Bastian's cock and slid his lips down the wet, straining shaft. Bastian's hands flew into his hair, and the movement was so sudden, Riley worried for a moment that he would be pulled away. The loud, drawn-out groan that followed told him quite the opposite. He worked his throat, swallowing and clenching a few times before bobbing his head. It made his head spin to move so much after feeding Bastian, but he didn't care.

His sole focus was giving Bastian the best damn orgasm of his life. He sucked hard, flicking his tongue over the head of Bastian's cock and following it with his teeth before taking him deep into his throat over and over. He brought one hand down to fondle and squeeze at Bastian's balls, and the sounds he pulled from Bastian shot up in pitch. Bastian's breath hitched, and Riley felt the thickness in his mouth swell ever so slightly. Bastian bucked, thrusting deep, and then a shout accompanied the rush of bittersweet fluid over his tongue.

He didn't stop there. Riley sucked and licked, moving down the length of Bastian's cock, and then nuzzled at his balls. He wanted to smother himself in the scent and warmth of Bastian's body. He'd missed it. God, he hadn't known just how much! He'd walked away from this, from everything he held dear. His home, his schooling, his cat, his lover. His cheeks burned with his shame, and he tilted his head back to look up at Bastian through wet lashes.

"I'm sorry," he said yet again. "Bastian... please..." What was he asking for? Absolution? Yes, forgiveness and love and the promise it'll be better for them from here on out.

Bastian was still panting, but he combed his fingers through Riley's hair and gently tugged at him. At first, Riley didn't know what Bastian wanted him to do. His confusion must have shown because a smile bloomed on Bastian's face, warm and sated. "Get up here so I can kiss you," Bastian ordered with another weak tug, and Riley complied immediately, rising enough for Bastian to seal their lips together. It was tender and possessive, all the things Riley could have possibly wanted in a kiss at that moment. Tears stung at his eyes again, and a soft sob escaped him when the kiss ended.

Bastian tugged at him again, and he followed until they were sprawled on the sofa. Bastian gathered him close, whispering, "It's all right, Riley. You're okay. You came back in time. I love you, and that's what's important." Bastian's arms squeezed him for a moment, almost like he expected him to disappear into thin air. "You nearly had me jumping out of my own skin. I was so worried about you. I drove myself crazy needing you, knowing you'd need my blood."

"I didn't know what I needed," Riley murmured, safe in Bastian's arms. "I tried to find it. I was so mad at you, I couldn't think straight. I love you, Bastian. I love you so much, but I did stupid things. I didn't know."

"I love you, too." The words were so important now, soaked in by both of them. His lips pressed to Riley's temple, Bastian asked, "Do you know what you need now?"

Riley smiled, tired and sore and feeling better than he had in weeks. "Yeah. You."

Coda

The blood on her tongue was sweet, everything she'd come to love of her Bonded. Add to it the sizzling glow following an explosive orgasm, and Havva was practically purring. As her Bonded cuddled against her side, Havva closed her eyes, thinking about her recent visitor.

"They are doing well, then, pretty one?" she asked.

The girl nodded against Havva's shoulder. "Riley's adjusting, and it'll take time, but I think they'll be all right."

"Perhaps. In time, they will realize that world is no longer theirs. It is *this* world they belong to."

Her Bonded sat up, blonde curls framing her round, flushed face. "They don't want this world."

Havva ran her fingers down her Bonded's face and throat, over the fresh bite there. "You did not either, lovely." She smiled, all teeth and sensual hunger. "But you have settled in nicely."

"Hard not to, once you worked your mojo on me." She shifted until she was straddling Havva, a lascivious grin on her face. "Of course, I've also come to appreciate the other benefits of the position."

Havva laughed at the euphemism. "Why talk around the obvious, child? Just say you like to fuck me."

"Mmm. Yes, very much."

"So you will continue to watch them for me? Be sure they are not doing anything *too* supremely stupid?"

"I would even if you didn't ask. I don't want them to fuck up, either. Riley's still my best friend. Nothing that's happened has changed that."

Havva brushed her fingertips along Cheryl's arms. "No," she said with a gentle sadness. "Not yet."

Other Works By S.L. Armstrong & K. Piet

The Keeper
Rachmaninoff
Catalyst
Alpha's Pride
Breaking Point

Other Works By S.L. Armstrong

Morningstar
Oneiros
Sacrifices (part of the *Daughters of Artemis* anthology)

Other Works By K. Piet

Surrender
The Fire of Her Eyes (part of the *Daughters of Artemis* anthology)

About the Authors

S.L. Armstrong has been writing for as long as she can remember. Art and reading have played a large part in her life since young childhood, but around fourteen, writing became her passion. Voraciously consuming every book in front of her opened up hundreds of worlds in her head, and she soon wanted to create worlds for other people as well. She has a particular fondness for gothic horror, horror, high fantasy, urban fantasy, and romance novels. The authors she turns to time and again are Stephen King, L.J. Smith, V.C. Andrews, R.L. Stine, and Anne Rice, among others. She has no shame in picking up the young adult novels she loved as a child, and she will talk your ear off about grammar and punctuation.

After she married her husband almost thirteen years ago, she began to truly delve into the world of writing for public consumption. It was sheer chance that she stumbled on M/M fanfiction, and she's not looked back. Though fanfiction will always have a fond place in her heart, she soon grew tired of playing in other people's sandboxes. When she discovered M/M romance, and how it was now a legitimate branch of romance writing, she knew her course. S.L. plans to release F/F, M/M, M/F, and multiple partner books as she continues her writing career. M/M romance is where her heart lies, no matter what else she may write or read, and it's where she keeps returning to.

There is something about two men passionately in love that just makes her heart melt, and she has no intention of giving that up anytime soon.

S.L. Armstrong lives in Florida with her husband, two dogs, and seven cats. She hates the heat and longs for a northern, snowy climate. She writes with K. Piet on a number of projects, but she also writes her own solitary titles as well. S.L. Armstrong owns Storm Moon Press LLC along with her husband and K. Piet, and she is proud of all they accomplish with the micro press.

K. Piet was born in California and raised in Flagstaff, Arizona, with her older sister and two cats. After studying in three different states and graduating magna cum laude from the University of Nevada – Las Vegas in Kinesiological Sciences, K. moved back to Flagstaff to pursue a career in therapeutic bodywork and massage. Her private massage business places an emphasis on sports massage for circus performers, dancers, and athletes training at high altitude.

Throughout high school and college, writing fiction was little more than a pleasant diversion from required essays and applied science courses. After working with author S. L. Armstrong on a number of small writing projects and coming to see the act of writing as a learned skill, K. found a new zeal for the challenge and now writes as a sideline career. She is particularly fond of writing in the High Fantasy and Paranormal genres, adding her own homoerotic, and often kinky, flair to her fiction.

She loves to hear from her readers, who can e-mail her at KPiet@kpiet.net.

www.ingramcontent.com/pod-product-compliance
Lightning Source LLC
Chambersburg PA
CBHW071132200626
46817CB00018B/2909